A Ride Down the Road

Betsy
Enjoy the ride! :)
— ♡ —

By Kourtney Govro

Edited by Erin Venable

©2019 All Rights Reserved

A Ride Down the Road ©2019

A Ride Down the Road ©2019

~ Chapter 1 ~

The car turned down the dusty driveway, her parents silent in the front seat Lucy leaned her head against the window and sighed. *"Weeks at Grandma's...... I may just as well crawl under a rock and die..."*

The scenery rolled by like a movie, as if it were not really outside the window of the car. Nothing but fields growing grass and edged by clusters of large trees. Not home. Not where her friends were located. Not where she wanted to be living for weeks. Outside, cows walked aimlessly through the field, munching on grass, their large bodies meandering across the open space without a care in the world. She imagined them having soft conversations with each other about the weather or something equally trivial, not knowing that, aside from her grandma, they would be her only living connection for who knows how long.

When she asked her parents how long she would be with her grandma, her mother had said that it would be long enough for her parents to "reconnect" and "figure things out". *What was there to figure out anyway?*

Part of her wanted them to just give up so she could join the ranks of the rest of the kids in her high school and have two Christmases and two birthdays. If they would get her a car, she wouldn't need to burden anyone with figuring out some schedule. She could just pick a house to sleep at... either one. She didn't care anymore. Anyway, it was only one more year till she got done with school and could leave for college. One more year...

Lining the road to her grandma's house were barbed wire fences laced with prickly blackberry vines and weeds, both plants intertwined and wrapping around the barbed wire as if they were one stem with two different kinds of leaves. At the end of the fence was a tall, branchy oak tree, perfect for climbing or supporting a tree house. She spent many hours last summer at its base, sketching in her book, its leafy branches shielding her from the scorching heat. The old tree arched over the street, dwarfing the small 3-bedroom farmhouse that sat on the other side of the road, its limbs scraping the top of the porch that spanned the length of the one-story house. The porch's red metal gliding chairs provided a pop of color against the house's crisp white siding and black shutters.

At the end of the porch hung a large swing, big enough to take naps on, complete with pillows and a quilt laid across its back. It looked like something out of a magazine, as if staged to invite guests to sit and enjoy a glass of lemonade with a friend.

A small woman knelt there in front, tending to the roses that graced the porch like jewelry on a fine lady. There were colors and textures rarely seen outside of a botanical garden.

As the car pulled up in front of the house, the woman nearly jumped to her feet, her floppy hat falling off and revealing pieces of silver hair sticking out of a scarf. Lucy had never seen an older woman move so quickly. Her red garden apron, sprinkled with white and yellow flowers, flapped open, revealing a faded blue dress. She pulled off a glove to wave with her bare hand, waddling across the front yard and down to the driveway in record speed.

"Hello!" she called waving and almost giggling as she made her way to the Suburban that had just pulled up in her drive. The sheer joy on her face made Lucy smile a bit. Lucy's mother jumped out of the car and ran across the yard.

"Mom! What are you doing?!"

Lucy followed slowly behind, with her father trailing the both of them.

"Well, these flowers aren't going to prune themselves, my dear." She said, hugging her daughter. "You look thin… What is wrong with you? Have you been eating?"

"Mom, I am the same size as the last time you saw me." The now gloveless, wrinkled hands began to squeeze Lucy's mother's arms as her smile turned into a look of concern. "Nonsense!" She said "You are melting to nothing. Like a sugar cube on a wet day! You need to eat. I made cookies."

With that, she turned from her daughter and grabbed Lucy's hands, clasping them in hers.

"Come now, let's go have some cookies. Cookies make things better, and I made a cake, too. That always helps!" She laughed and put her arm around Lucy. "Let's go snack and catch up a bit. When we're at church, we call this 'fellowship,' but here, we just call it 2pm or whatever time the clock says. It's always good to have a snack." Lucy looked at her mom with an "Oh, my word, take me home, please, NOW!" look.

Inside the house, the smell of chocolate chip cookies and peanut butter cake filled the large, rectangular family room. A floral couch and two blue easy chairs sat against the wall facing an outdated TV, which was housed in an ornate wooden cabinet, the speakers on the side. In the middle of each brown speaker cover was a black metal diamond with a star inside.

On top of the TV cabinet sat five large picture frames, each one holding what looked like a high school senior picture of a smiling teen. Lucy recognized her mom in one of the pictures, with her unmistakable smile and fluffy black hair, held in place by a blue headband. Her eyes were so dark that you couldn't see the pupils, her cheeks perfectly pink. Other pictures were scattered around the room, covering every surface, most of them of Lucy's aunts, uncles, and other family members.

As Lucy surveyed the cluttered mess of pictures, there was one that stood out: A young woman with black hair standing next to a man and an old truck. In the back of the truck were two young boys, one in overalls with no shirt wearing a straw cowboy hat and the other in a button-down shirt and pants. All were smiling and seemed to be having the perfect day. The woman was wearing a form-fitting dress but seemed a little heavy, maybe even pregnant. The man was tall and broad, his button-down shirt ironed stiff. The date on the back of the photo was 1954, but the couple looked oddly familiar.

Her grandma's voice interrupted Lucy's reverie, and she quickly set the picture down in its place. "Lucy, what will you have? I have cake, cookies, and fudge, or if you go pick some black berries, I will make you a pie."

Oh my gosh...is this my whole summer? I am going to gain a million pounds! Lucy thought as she walked into the small kitchen.

"How about you grab the bucket from the barn and go for a walk. Let me catch up with your mom, her grandma said. Her mom had that look again... the one that Lucy hated... the one that said, "I might cry and don't want you to see."

Lucy looked at her mom and smiled softly, wanting her to know that it would be okay and that she was alright, even though she wasn't... even though she *didn't* want two Christmas' and two birthdays... even though she just wanted things to go back to normal... But she knew her mom knew that.

"Go on sweetheart – there are black berries in the backyard, so you don't have to go too far." Lucy's mom sat down at the kitchen table and picked up a cookie as Grandma pulled a glass bottle of milk from the fridge. It was like the kitchen was frozen in time. There was a small round maple table with 4 matching chairs. Lucy was convinced they were for people of small stature, although her Grandfather had never seemed to be anything but large, with broad shoulders and a barrel chest. He had died only a year ago, and she missed his quiet ways and gentle smile. Lucy gave a forced smile. "Yes ma'am," she sighed, as she trudged off to the barn, her

A Ride Down the Road ©2019

red Converse sneakers tracing a colorful path through the grass.

Lucy wasn't much of the status quo type - she marched to her own drum. She was an artist and like to sketch and paint. She could sit for hours and look at things… like an explorer from the seven seas, she would study an object or person's face, and then recreate it in her book. Not that it would do her any good past high school, but she did like to relax with her sketch pad.

She remembered to wear jeans this time, a lesson learned on her last visit when she had torn her favorite pair of Umbro shorts. They were the only pair she had with the actual logo, rather than just some cheap knock-off from Wal-Mart. The kids at school made fun of her when she wore her "fake" shorts, and she acted like it didn't bother her. Heavy and out-of-fashion were not a good combination for high school. But over the summer, she had grown taller and lost weight, learning to tame her wavy brown hair and put on makeup. It was quite an accomplishment for an awkward 16-year-old.

The green grass around the barn was thick and a little tall, in need of a trim, even though the ground felt hard and dry beneath it. The barn's red exterior was weather-worn and the silver, rusted metal roof looked as if it needed repair. To some, it might seem creepy, but Lucy always found it a bit inviting. To her, it had a story to tell.

Last summer, she sat in the hay loft and sketched. It was there that she first heard her parents arguing. They were good about hiding it at home, and they assumed they were being discreet by going to the barn. They didn't know she was there, just above them, listening in despair as her mother cried and explained how she didn't know how to go on and pretend anymore, that her heart was broken. Her father seemed to be trying to explain, searching for words to make her understand. He wasn't good with words. He often got lost in his thoughts and would drift off for hours of silent thinking. Lucy was convinced he did math problems for fun and that his mind was always in motion, making calculations

A Ride Down the Road ©2019

and solving equations. Her mom, on the other hand, used lots of words… too many… every conversation was heavily weighted on her side. They went back and forth (mostly forth from her mother, with very little back from her father) until Lucy knocked over her cup of colored pencils, bringing the heated conversation to a sudden halt. When they saw her sitting there, her mother ran from the barn, her father watching her leave without a word. Then he sadly looked at his feet and walked out.

A barn cat brushed against her leg and purred pulling her out of her memory and back to reality. She turned to look through the yard to find the bucket. It was hooked to a water pump connected to a long, metal raceway that led to a metal tub on the other side of the barbed wire. She pumped it. Nothing. Pump pump pump. It was no use. Her mind had this idea that if she put in enough effort, it might work - that's what happens when you really try, that things get better if you put in the work. Like her parents' marriage. That if they just kept trying and working and... pumping. Pump pump. But still no water.

Irritated, she kicked the bucket across the yard, then watched it roll across the grass and come to rest at the feet of none other than her father.

"What are you doing?" he asked

"Nothing," she said, looking at her feet. The white part of her sneakers had some green on them from walking across the yard. "I thought if I tried it, then it would work."

She looked up at her dad. He was tall and thin. His glasses were thick. His hair was light brown and eyes green like the grass… just like Lucy's. He always wore a button-down shirt, even to do yard work. He never just put on a T-shirt and jeans - it was always some different variations of a button-down shirt or, in the winter, a flannel. He often wore long white socks with his shorts and tennis shoes, which would normally embarrass any teenager, but not Lucy. She seemed to get her quirkiness from him.

He ran his hand through his wavy hair.

"Sometimes things don't work, no matter what you do," he said as he walked over to the pump. He put his hand on it as if to push the pump, but stopped and put his hands in his pockets, looking intently at Lucy. "Why don't you *try,* Dad? If you could try to make things work, then..." she pleaded, her eyes coming away from her shoes and up to his face. They stared at each other, both knowing that life was changing whether her parents got a divorce or not. The years would come and go, and then Lucy would be off to college. Nothing they could do would stop the train from leaving the station.

"I am *trying* to make things work with your mother," he said, awkwardly. "It's not like I have given up... I think this will help us mend things," and then rambled on for a bit about how difficult things had become in their marriage. Looking at her intently, he insisted again, "Lucy, I *am* trying." His hand gripped the pump as he tried to reassure his daughter, and suddenly, with one pump, water gushed out and down the raceway to the metal tub. Lucy knew that if they were really trying to make things work it would be like the pump....but she wasn't confident that was the case.

A Ride Down the Road ©2019

~ Chapter 2 ~

The rooster crowing outside of her room was an unwelcome alarm clock. Lucy was sure that it delighted in coming to her window to wake her up. She uncovered her head. "Stupid bird," she said out loud. She stared at the ceiling, the fan turning slowly above her as it moved the air through the room.

Three days, 25 cookies, one piece of cake, and four pieces of fudge had passed since her parents left. She sat up in bed and reached over to the nightstand for her glasses, knocking an oval-shaped clock to the floor. Its gold rimmed frame, with glowing arms and numbers sitting on an avocado-colored base, gave it a retro look that was probably highly sought after in some fancy decorator stores. She picked it up quickly, setting it back on the nightstand. There, next to the lamp and the old clock was a small picture of her grandpa. She sleepily picked it up to take a closer look.

Lucy smiled as she studied the photo. Her grandpa was Spanish with dark eyes and defined features, the very definition of "tall, dark and handsome." She sure didn't get those striking features. She took after her dad. She was fair-skinned and freckled, with light brown hair that hinted of red in the sun. She had a heart-shaped face, with a widow's peak on her forehead.

She set the picture back down and shuffled down the hallway. The door to her grandma's room was open, the bed neatly made. The multicolored feed sack quilt had wide yellow trim and dozens of small squares in various patterns. Every morning, it was the same: a bed made like a hotel and a perfectly set room.

Lucy wandered down the hallway to the kitchen where a plate of biscuits sat covered by a small tea towel and a plate of ham. She made herself a sandwich and sat down. Through the front widow she saw her grandma sitting on the

A Ride Down the Road ©2019

swing, legs covered in a blue quilt with white trim, Bible laying open on her lap. Every morning, it was the same breakfast on the table, with Grandma out on the porch.

As Lucy got up and poured herself a cup of coffee, she stopped by the TV to look once again at the picture of the couple with the two boys.   Convinced that the two boys looked familiar, she scanned the photo for some kind of hint, finally deciding to just ask her grandma instead.

Lucy headed for the porch, then sat down next to her grandma.

"Well, hello did the rooster wake you again?" she said with a giggle. "He is a good alarm clock. He does not let the day get away from us."

Lucy nodded and shrugged, then slowly pulled the picture out to show her grandma. "Is this you and Grandpa?" she asked. Grandma took the picture and smiled, running her fingers over the picture of the young woman. "No, no dear…that's not me. It was my best friend. Her name was Grace. The curse of growing old is your friends beat you to heaven. Grace lived with your Grandpa and I when she came to Radical. That is what this town used to be called. She was my cousin and were very close."

"Why did she come to Radical?"

"Her mother died, and her father had left long before that happened. She was alone, and we were a safe place to land. When we were young, she would spend summers with me and my family at the sea. We lived by the ocean - she loved it there with us. She said it was clean and quiet. We wrote letters through the year, and she was even in my wedding. When her mother died, she had nowhere to go, so we took her in."

Lucy stared at the picture. "So, those are her boys?"

"Well… that's an interesting story…

A Ride Down the Road ©2019

Her grandma got up and touched her arm, motioning towards the house.

"Let's get a cookie." Lucy followed her in.

Grandma went to her room and came out carrying an old creme puff box. It was red and tan with worn edges, and in it were letters tied with twine and small journal. She explained that, when Grace passed away, her children brought the box to her. She had, in turn, placed the letters she had written to Grace in the same box so that when she died, someone would be able to read the letters and piece together the whole story. Under the pile of letters was a picture of the two women sitting together, having a picnic under a tree.

Lucy pulled out the journal and opened it up. As she read the words, the scene played out in her mind...

The train whistle blew, and Grace could feel it slowing to a stop. The train was plush and wood on the walls. The windows had offered a gallery of landscapes, like paintings flashing by scene by scene. She took a deep breath... this was the start of her new life. The end of a journey across the country to a new beginning. She grasped her green velvet bag and ran her fingers back and forth over the beading. It was one of the few possessions she had from her mother.

The daughter of a stage actress, she had lived behind the curtains as her mother would sing for crowds full of fine ladies and men dressed for evenings of entertainment. She would sit in the back and listen, admiring her mother from afar. Tall and lean, her mother was statuesque with a perfectly formed silhouette. She was flawless in every hand-picked ornate outfit. The ruffles and beading made her mother look rich, and after her stage time she fit in seamlessly with the fine people who visited. Her perfect black hair was always held in place with a brilliant jeweled clip, the very clip that Grace had sold to buy a ticket West to live with her cousin, Laura. It was in the shape of a leaf, the edges gold with inlaid green stones, one of the few things she had left after the fire that took everything but what was stored in her mother's dressing room at the theatre. It even took her beautiful and talented mother, which was a nightmare that seemed to never stop. Penniless and homeless, all she had to her name was a small picture and the little green velvet handbag. The owners of the theatre reached out to her cousin:

Dear Christopher & Laura

We regret to inform you that Pearl McCombs has been killed in a fire, leaving behind her daughter, Grace. We have kept her for these past few days using the remaining pay owed to her mother to support her. We will help her get a train ticket and get to your home.   Grace is a strong young woman willing to work and support herself.

They didn't know… they didn't know that Laura was the only person in the world that Grace loved as much as she loved her mother.   She overheard them tell the others how they were generously taking care of her.

It's a strange thing to be unwanted by the ones who acted as though they loved her mother so much… Grace was convinced that their love was for all the money her mother made for them. Grace was not as beautiful as her mother, by any means. "Plain" is how the theatre owners described her to others. "How could Pearl's child be so plain?" they would say. The stage manager had once told her it must be hard to be the daughter of such a beautiful woman. Grace's hair was dark brown but not black like night. It was wavy and not sleek like her mother's.   Her skin was freckled… not porcelain like her mother's.   And she could not sing… at least not like her mother. In fact, *most* of her thoughts about herself ended with the phrase "not like her mother". The only common thing was their bright green eyes. Grace loved her mother's eyes… no one had the same image in their mind of them because they were special when they looked at Grace.
  Eyes, you see, are funny things… they speak without

words. A glance that said "I love you" is what Grace missed the most.

Regardless of what anyone else thought of Grace, her mother looked at her as if she was the most beautiful girl in the world. She would say "No other creation, whether on earth or in the heavens, would ever be as special as you, my Sweet One. Nothing as beautiful."

The train stopped in a city called St. Louis, and a businessman boarded. He seemed bothered that the only open seat was next to her. Reluctantly, he plopped down next to her. He was not a talker. Grace tried to engage him a few times, his replies short and gruff.   He was middle-aged, wearing a black suit and tie. He held a newspaper and seemed engrossed in its every word. She cocked her head to the side and inconspicuously read the article on the cover. It was the story of the new governor of Missouri. "What must it be like to be a governor and have to move to a home to live in for a period of time?" she thought. The article said he had a wife and three children. One son and two daughters. He and his wife and leave their home to live in the Governor's mansion. His name was Henry Carter, and he was a Democrat. Grace was not sure what that meant. His son would take over the family business, a bank in Springfield.

As Grace peered at her seatmate, she couldn't help but think how uncomfortable it must be to wear a tie all day. She studied the tie -- it seemed to pinch his neck slightly below his collar as though it twisted his skin a bit and the tie was holding the skin in place. She heard a grunt and awkwardly looked up to see his dark eyes glaring at her. His mustache twitched like a flag in the wind.

"Oh, I am sorry… I was reading your newspaper and seem to have been staring… I apologize," she said, hoping he would engage in conversation. No luck. Mostly, she wanted to ask him what the word "democrat" meant and why the governor's family had to live in Jefferson City, but she had a feeling that it was not the right time.

She quickly looked away and out the window at the hills rolling past them. They were covered in trees which made them look soft, as if you could walk on them. They were so close together she wondered if you could actually walk through the woods, what with all the trees. Green and bumpy contrasted with the bright blue sky. On occasion they would cross through a field where cows would graze in the open valley and she could see them wandering towards tufts of uneaten grass. "It must be nice to be like that -- only wandering to your next meal and knowing it would be there," she thought. "But I guess maybe not wonderful when you become dinner," she giggled to herself. This was nothing like the city or the sea, but she would be content in anything.

She leaned her head against the window as the train stopped. This was it... a new beginning and a new life. "Lord, help me," she said under her breath as she gazed off in the distance. She didn't want to move, because movement would make the moment real. She was not ready for real. She had only read about the West and all she knew she gained from her cousins' letters. Laura described the hills as mountains in her letters and said that they were beautiful but could be treacherous. In the summer, they were lush and green, dense and thick. In the fall, the trees would turn into a menagerie of color: orange, yellow, red, and all shades in between. The color was more beautiful than anything Laura had ever seen. It made missing the sea less challenging because the hills were so lovely. There was a river. Laura said the water was clear and cold. Grace let her mind paint the picture. "It will be ok, and I will be happy," she sighed. "Lord, hear my prayer," she begged in a soft, audible voice.

A man in a train conductor hat tapped Grace on the shoulder, saying, "Ms. Grace, isn't this your stop?" She looked up, realizing the car was empty. "Oh, my! Oh, yes... I am sorry." She fumbled with her hat as she jumped to her feet and grabbed her book. "Thank you, Charlie." Grace, never one to meet a stranger, had befriended Charlie on the long journey. Charlie had ridden trains for as long as he could remember. He knew the ins and outs and was chatty

A Ride Down the Road ©2019

with his new, young friend.   Charlie's wrinkled face smiled as he patted her arm. "It will be a wonderful journey, young lady. Remember there is always a plan... even when it does not feel like it."

Grace nodded, shook his hand warmly, and rushed off the train, forgetting the stairs. As she tumbled down to the ground, she felt a man catch her. "Was it the man with the mustache?" she thought. "Now he will think I am crazy *and* clumsy!"

 "Oh, my!" she exclaimed as he steadied her, looking as surprised as she was. "I am terribly sorry!"

"It's quite alright. Are you Grace?" She looked at the man, not quite knowing what to say. His blue eyes smiled a warm greeting, just like her mother's used to do.

"GRACE!" She heard a familiar voice as her cousin Laura ran up to greet her with a warm hug. Finally, someone who felt like home. Laura was a small woman with blond hair. She had high cheekbones and bright blue eyes. She grew up just outside the city, and Grace's fondest memories were of going to spend warm summer months with her, close to the sea. Laura's father was Pearl's brother. She was the closest thing that Grace had to a sibling. They wrote each other weekly, and Grace heard all about the town where her husband, Christopher, served as a minister.   Her letters would tell tales of Christopher going into the hills to look for people to invite to their small church.

As they walked arm in arm, Christopher followed close behind. He was tall, a rather intimidating figure with broad shoulders and black curly hair. His family was from Southern Spain. His father was a ship maker who came to the US for work when he was 10 years old. His parents had not been thrilled when Christopher decided to attend a protestant church, and were even less happy when he let them know he wanted to be a pastor in the Midwest.

"I am so glad to be here," Grace said, exhaling as she stepped back and looked at her cousin. Laura was rounded in the middle, pregnant with her first baby. Grace paused for a moment, looking gratefully at her cousin, as Laura gently touched her cheek and said, "Come my sweet. Here is home. You are home... *this* is your home. We are glad you are here."

~ Chapter 3 ~

Five days, 35 cookies, three pieces of cake, and four pieces of fudge had passed since her parents left… plus biscuits, gravy, ham, green beans made with bacon fat, and all sorts of other grandma-level things. Lucy had started to question her decision to pack pants that zip and button rather than those with elastic waist bands and spandex. Oh, well… it seemed to soothe her soul and made her miss her parents less. To counteract the overindulgence, Lucy would wander the property while her grandma napped.

Her grandma kept encouraging her to call out to God with her burdens… Lucy wondered why, if God really cared about her burdens, did He seem to give her so many. "Why can't you just swoop in and fix this? If you are 'sovereign' and 'all-powerful', why can't You just take a moment and fix this? My parents should just stay married! God, if You care about me, why can't You just fix this?" Her "whys" grew angrier as she walked 'til she finally threw her hands up. She was in the middle of nowhere. She chuckled to herself, realizing that loneliness had become her only friend. She missed her *real* friends: Jamie, with her careful, thoughtful answers, Lisa and her warm friendliness, and even Torrie, the sweet friend who always seemed to be in her own world. When Lucy told her friends about the potential divorce, Torrie quickly told her, "God won't give you more than you can handle." Jamie corrected her, noting that the oft-touted phrased was not really in the Bible, and Lisa hugged her, telling her to ignore them both. Lucy had responded, irritated, "God will never give me more than I can handle all by myself? That's totally crap – I have more than I can handle all the time!" Jamie tried to be thoughtful and patted her friend's back. "It would be illogical for God to *not* give you more than you could handle, because it proves you need Him."

Lucy looked up at the sky as she replayed the conversation in her head. "This is definitely more than I can handle…" she sighed, pushing open the gate and wandering out into the pasture. The fields were open, the tall grass rolling like brown and green waves. Lucy walked through it, letting her hands be tickled by the tops of the blades. There was a patch of trees in the middle of the field, and Lucy tossed her blanket down under a tree, unpacking her picnic basket filled with snacks, her sketch pad, pencils, the letters, and the journal. She stretched out on her stomach and looked through her pictures… the one of her grandma on the swing made her smile. She was convinced that she captured joy the way her eyes creased at the sides, the deep lines around her mouth, and even the way her jawline drooped just a little. The deeper the lines in a person's face, the more of the journey that person had enjoyed. Grandma was in her 80s… her journey had obviously been good. The next was a picture of the train that Grace rode on… or at least what she imagined the train looked like. The steam, the rivets, the wheels… even the man in the small black hat who took the tickets. As she looked at it closely, she giggled, because it also resembled the train from the Harry Potter movie, which was her only frame of reference of a *real* train. She almost penciled in the boy with the lighting bolt on his head but then stopped herself.

Lucy rolled over and stared at the sky through the trees, then pulled out the journal.   Grace's handwriting was so beautiful -- the letters curled and connected. It was almost like one of Lucy's drawings. The entries went from describing situations and people to letters to God.

Our school room is always noisy early in the morning, like the sea as it approaches high tide. The children seem to get more and more antsy as the clock nears time to sit… like seagulls on the beach when we feed them scraps of bread.

"Alright, alright," Laura called, clapping her hands. The ten children shuffled to their places and pulled out their books. She wasn't taller than the oldest boy, who was 15. The new legislation said the youngest a child could leave school was 15. If the children wanted to go beyond what their little town had to offer they had to travel to the next town. Laura was tiny and delicate with a perfect round bump.   She was due in a few weeks, which meant Grace would be taking over the class until she could return, even though Grace wasn't sure how she would manage without her.

Laura began to teach, starting the younger kids on an exercise of alphabets and numbers, then working her way through to the older kids. Each group worked on different problems and projects. Grace admired her ability to manage so many kids and so many different capacities.

"Albert, where is your brother? She asked a small, strawberry blonde-haired boy in the front of the classroom. Grace loved Albert. He often would come sit with her during lunch and talk with her about the birds or the sky.   His eyes were blue and his face freckled. He was joyful and funny. His brother Benjamin looked like an older version of the same person aside from the fact that he was three years older, you would have thought they were twins. Ben walked Albert to and from school daily. It was surprising to see one without the other. "He is…um…not here. He is with my Dad." Laura frowned and patted his head.

In the last few weeks, Grace had learned all the kids' names and tried to learn about their families. The 15-year-old Garrett twins, Kevin and Tanner, were the oldest kids at the school. They often coordinated games and activities for the rest of the students.   Their parents owned the store in town, so they always had new shoes and were well-dressed. Their younger sister, Stella, was beautiful and very well-spoken for a 12-year-old. She was kind and observant, always helping the younger ones with their work. John-Michael was 10 and rather outspoken. He was a heavy-set boy who would probably become monstrously large someday, like his father. He was the youngest, the last one to go through the school. His three older brothers made it to 15 and left school to help their father, and his two sisters had gone to high school in the next town. They would often stop by the school on their way back to town to walk him home. Their family farm, the largest in the county, was just past Albert's home, and it was expected that the whole family pitched in to work. Grace had heard that John Michael's father had wanted more children -- a great labor force of workers -- but his mother said that after John-Michael, God broke the mold.

The Hopkins, Bradleys, and Bolls, rounded out the rest of the rowdy crew. Grace was always fascinated by how different each child looked, yet how similar. Coming from New York, she had known such a variety of people that the homogenous crowd here seemed bland. Her mother's theatre had guests from all over the world, and Grace would listen to their conversations with the theatre owners, often in broken English, then hear them speak to each other in their native tongue. It was incredible how different things were here.

The day went on, and Laura seemed to dance across the front of the classroom as she shared and taught. The students loved her, and she loved them. She knew their names, their abilities, their learning styles, and their habits. She could tell if they were out-of-sorts from fatigue or stress. She often went to the Garretts' to petition for some needed item, or she'd make them herself. "No one should have holes in their shoes in the winter… we are all too blessed to let that happen," she would write in her letters to Grace. Finally seeing all of these children, who had previously been nothing but figments of her imagination, helped Grace understand Laura's drive to care for and love each one.

As the day went on, Laura grew tired. She sat down in a chair, hands on the sides of her baby bump, and taught the final lesson. The class seemed to sense that their beloved leader was wearing down and kept themselves in line. When the older kids noticed the younger kids acting out, they would step in and help corral them. "Class dismissed," she said. "Albert, come here, please." As the children gathered their things, Albert skipped to her. She whispered in his ear, and he seemed pleased. He went and packed his bag.

"Grace," Laura called from her chair "Would you mind walking Albert home? His father can probably drive you back. I need to get home and rest." Grace smiled and walked up to Albert, who reached up and grabbed her hand.

"Of course, Albert and I always have such fun conversations." Albert beamed with excitement as they left the school and headed down the road, hand-in-hand. They walked with an energetic John-Michael, who rattled on and on about a book he was reading that talked about bugs.

"I like the green bugs the best… because you can't see them and they could jump out… and BITE YOU!" he yelled, raising his arms and jumping at Albert. Albert winced and hid behind Grace's arm.

"John-Michael, do you ever catch bugs and put them in a cage? One of my mom's friends in New York talked about how, where he was from, they would fry the bugs and eat them!" Grace chimed in above his head. Both boys made an ewww face and snickered. "They said they are a delicacy. Though I can't imagine a friend bug being very delicate. Albert, could you eat a bug?"

Albert thought for a moment, then squeezed her hand. "I don't think so…" he said sheepishly crinkling his freckled nose and looking up at his friend. "I think they would be too squishy or something… yuck!" He said moving his mouth as if something disgusting had made it past his lips and offended his delicate palate t.

John-Michael and Albert started playing tag and running around in front of Grace as she walked. She looked out at the fields, waving around them like green oceans, and her heart grew wistful for the sea. The wind blew and the wheat billowed side to side. She imagined ships, like those in the harbor, making their way across the brownish green sea of wheat, and seagulls, rather than song birds, flying by to wish her hello. She was so engrossed in her vision of wonder that she tripped over Albert and they both went tumbling.

"Oh, goodness!" she exclaimed, as she and the little boy hit the ground. She was concerned she had hurt him, then heard his giggles. John-Michael put his hands on his knees and cackled at the sight. "You two fell down!" he called, and he sat down as if his laughter had taken so much out of him that he could no longer stand. The trio laughed, not hearing the approaching car until it was right behind them. Grace jumped to her feet and grabbed Albert's arm, quickly yanking him up. The car stopped, and out stepped a man in a suit. Grace froze. She didn't recognize him and wasn't sure why he would be stopping.

"Are you all right?" he said, quickly coming around the front of the beautiful car. Grace had never seen anything so fine. In New York, you would occasionally see vehicles, but those all seemed to be older than this one.

Grace quickly wiped her hands on her skirt.

"Yes, yes…. just a bit clumsy…" she said, regretting the laughter. "We're fine."

The man was now standing in front of her, seeming to survey the lot. He had on a pinstriped suit and a fine black hat. She had seen people in New York in fancy clothes like this, but nothing of the like here, at least not since she had arrived. He was a just a bit taller than her, and lean. His eyeglasses were round and sat close to his face. She was so taken with how dashing he seemed in his suit that she stopped talking and just stared. He seemed to be doing the same.

"James Carter," he said, quickly putting out his hand to shake hers. She took it gently. "I am from Springfield and coming through town to meet with Mr. Bradley."

"Bradley's farm is next to my house," Albert said, stepping between the stranger and Grace. "I'm Albert." Albert then stuck his dirty hand out for the man to shake. It worked, and the man smiled.

"Albert, nice to meet you – is this your mom?" Grace must have made a face and the man turned red, as Albert laughed. "No, this is Ms. Grace -- she is my teacher. My mom is not here anymore."

John-Michael began to laugh again, putting his hands on his knees and rolling on the ground. "You thought she was his mom?! She's the *teacher*... and she's *not* married."

Grace, burning with embarrassment at how her marital status had been disclosed, shot him a look, and he quickly stopped laughing. He turned instead to look sheepishly down the long driveway. "Well, this is my stop. See you tomorrow, Albert. Bye, Ms. Grace!" With that, John-Michael ran down the street towards his house, where -- Grace was sure -- he would be welcomed by a mountain of manual labor and immense teasing from his older brothers. "Manual labor is good for that one," Grace thought to herself as his words still hung in the air, making her cheeks hot. "He needs something to get his mind focused!" "Well," said Grace, turning to smile uncomfortably at James, "We should be going – I was just walking Albert home." She gently nudged Albert to start walking down the dirt street, wondering how much dust was actually on her face. How embarrassed she was to be seen sitting in the dirt after a fall!

"Wait!" James said, reaching out and touching her arm. "I can drive you. Albert, you said it was on the way, right?" Albert nodded as he eyed the fancy car and started to walk towards it. Grace quickly grabbed his arm.

"Oh, we couldn't impose. I mean, we both just fell in the dirt, and I would hate to get your car dirty."

James chuckled and smiled at her. "It's a car, not a museum. It's not worth anything if I can't help someone. Please, I wouldn't think of having you walk." Albert looked at Grace with wide begging eyes and took her hand.

"All right then," she said. Albert let go of her hand and ran to the car. It was shiny and black with a hood ornament perched right in the center. The front of the car was sleek and had round, bubbly edges. It was a Dodge, with white wall tires and striking silver trim. Albert touched the hood and looked back at James and Grace, then ran to the back door and jumped in. Grace lowered her head a bit and walked towards the passenger door. James quickly went around her and opened the door.

"*You* should never open a door… never…" he smiled at her as she sat carefully in the seat then pulled in both legs. She had never seen anything like it. The dashboard was a warm wood with a metal inlay. There was a clock that looked like the one she had next to her bed and a speedometer. It even had a radio. She was enamored by all of the knobs and pulls. James came around the car and hopped into the driver's seat.

"It's brand new. I just got it off the lot last week. I drive to a lot of places for work, and it's very helpful to have such a nice car." He rattled on about the car, but Grace was so captivated by its beauty that she didn't listen. She reached and ran her hand across the beautiful dash. Suddenly realizing she was not paying attention, she stopped and looked at James. He was smiling at her… "You are beautiful," he said, then looked as if he were surprised at himself for his sudden directness.

"Thank you," she said, looking at her hands. Albert started asking questions in the back, which was a welcome distraction for Grace. She didn't know what to say now that he had said *that* to her.

"What do you do that you have such a nice car?" Albert asked, as James started the car and headed down the road.

"I work at a bank… actually, my father *owns* the bank, but he's no longer working there. He's found himself another job he likes better, at least for the moment. right now."

"He just up and left his job, just like that?!" Albert inquired in a young, surprised voice.

"Well, he got a better job. And he decided I could run the bank on my own," James said, smiling. Grace couldn't figure out what to say and just kept looking at the dashboard and out the window. "It's hard work running a bank," he continued. "But it's what I went to school for and got an education in. Education is really important, Albert. If you don't get one, you will end up as a farmer and always owe someone something..." He paused, as Albert seemed puzzled, and Grace was looking at him now. "So, Albert, what do you like to do for fun? Do you help on your father's farm?"

"Well, some. Not too much. I cook some and help at the house. We don't have a mom at home anymore."

"Did she pass away?" James asked, as matter-of-factly as he could without sounding cold. Grace was curious as to how Albert would answer. She had never asked about his mother, she just assumed she was at home. His father, David, had been to their house several times to drop off produce or meat for the pastor. He had even been over to help fix the door when the hinge broke. Grace had never wondered where his wife was before. Maybe that was wrong... but she just assumed she was at home.

"No, she left. She didn't want to be with us anymore." Albert said, seeming sad, but without emotion, like a blank piece of paper. "She just wanted to go home to St. Louis, but that was when I was a little boy. I don't remember her very much."

The car was silent for a bit, with only the rumble of the engine daring to make any noise. As they neared the farm, Grace pointed, and Albert called out, "There's where I live, over there!"

"I really appreciate the ride. It was really kind of you." Grace said

"I wonder," James said, as they neared the house, "I am going to be in this area for a few days... would you want to have dinner with me some evening?"

Grace smiled and looked at her hands again, then over at the driver. James held tightly to the large steering wheel, looking straight ahead, seeming to brace for rejection.

"I would love that," she said. "I live at the parsonage with my cousin. If you would like to call on me there, I would enjoy seeing you."

The car pulled up in front of the house and Albert jumped out, running up to Grace's side of the vehicle.

"A *lady* should *not* open a door," he said, winking at James, who nodded with approval.

Grace stepped out and turned, grabbing the door before Albert could slam it shut.

"I look forward to seeing you, Mr. Carter."

"Wait," he called out, as she turned to go, "What is your full name?"

"Grace *McCombs* -- my last name is McCombs" she said, smiling as she closed the door. She then turned and walked with Albert towards the farmhouse. James sat pensively in the car, watching as they walked hand-in-hand, then quietly drove off.

As they drew near to the house, Ben came barreling out of the garage towards his brother and Grace.

"Hello, Ms. Grace!" he cried out excitedly, running up to her and hugging her waist so tight she lost her breath.

"Hello, Ben!" she said, rubbing his goldish red locks and looking down at him, then grabbing his face in her hands. "Why were you not at school today?"

"That was my fault." She heard a voice nearing and looked up to see a taller version of the boys. David neared the group, his reddish skin freckled from the sun under his rolled-up shirt sleeves. He had been working all day in the barn and sweat and dirt covered his clothes and face. "I needed some help today and John-Michael's brothers were tied up with a few things. I thought keeping him home for one day wouldn't be too much to ask. The cow had a baby, and it's just hard to manage all that and everything else alone." He smiled, and the boys took off towards the barn to see the new calf. "Would you like to see?" he asked, nodding his head towards the barn.

Grace smiled back. "Yes, of course!" she replied, laughing as they walked to the large red barn behind the white farmhouse. The barn was full of hay, and in the back was a large cow and small calf. The boys hung on the fence, looking at the small animal. To them, it was a pet, not a future meal.

"I can drive you back," David said. "It's the least I can do for you walking Albert home."

"We didn't walk the whole way… a man in a car picked us up. He was going to the Bradleys' -- says he's from the bank."

A bit of concern flashed briefly on David's face. "Bradley's farm?"

"Yes. He said he was coming by for a visit clear from Springfield. His Dad used to run the bank, but he left that job for a different one, apparently."

"Governor… his dad is the governor – you met James Carter."

A Ride Down the Road ©2019

~ Chapter 4 ~

Six days later, Lucy started to lose count of cookies, pieces of cake, and pieces of fudge. Grandma shared her secret stash of frozen Snickers bars after dinner one night. They laughed as they chopped the candy to pieces and sprinkled it on homemade ice cream.

"Grandma, do you want to see my sketch book?"

"Of course!" her Grandma said, as she quickly scraped the sides of the bowl to get the last bits of delight from its edges. Lucy pulled her chair up next to her grandma's recliner and opened up her book, sitting her bowl on the small, round end table.

"Oh! That's me!" Grandma said, looking intently at the picture. "Do you really think I look *that* old?"

Lucy stuttered over her response, worried she had hurt her grandma's feelings. "No, you don't look old," she said. "It's probably just lighting…" Her Grandma looked at her sternly and raised her eyebrows, then started to giggle. "Oh, sweet one, I know I am old." They both laughed as Lucy quickly turned the page. She showed her the train, and Lucy explained how it was like Harry Potter. She then explained *who* Harry Potter was and why it was in a movie. Lucy then flipped to the picture of the car that picked up Grace. Grandma's brow furled as she reached for the page to change it to the next picture. Then last picture was David's truck.

Grandma touched the sketch of the old truck.

"David was so kind… so kind…" She said, her voice trailing off. "You will never really be able to understand that from anything written by any of us. He cared for your grandpa and me when we lost our first son… before Grace even came to town, I lost a little boy. We were devastated. I never even told her about it until years later. I don't know why... if I was embarrassed or if I was just private and didn't want to show all the emotion that went along with the loss of a child. But David... he showed up daily with food and helped around the house. He had his own work to do, but he always came to our aide. If the church ever needed anything, he just quietly took care of it... no pomp or circumstance...just quietly enabled the ministry. He was a wonderful man."

"How did you meet him?" Lucy asked, looking at her drawing, wondering if she could find a description in Grace's journal or letters about David.

"When he lost his wife... well, she wasn't lost exactly anyway... he was struggling. Two little boys and no help... he struggled. And my husband spent hours going out and helping him on the farm, encouraging him, and turning him away from the bottle and towards the Lord.   The Holy Spirit got ahold of that man, that's for sure."

Lucy smiled. She wondered why David was alone if he was so wonderful. The journal said that Albert told Grace their mom had left. If he was so wonderful, why would she leave?
  Ending a marriage over what? Was he mean, or maybe he was a drunk? What makes that happen, anyways? She realized that she may be wondering more for her parents than about this faceless person from Lucy's journals and her grandma's memory. Her parents didn't seem to have any of those issues either... maybe people just quit wanting to be married sometimes.

Grandma yawned and Lucy hopped up, taking their bowls to the kitchen for cleaning. When she tried to follow Grandma into her room, she was waved away.   "Dear heart, I love you but I don't need anyone seeing me without my face or my teeth," she chuckled, as she walked to the bathroom to prepare for bed. Lucy giggled -- the small plastic box in the bathroom that housed her grandma's teeth had scared her the night before when she was looking for some dental floss. She had opened the box and almost dropped the full set on the floor.   Who stores their teeth in a plastic little tub? Apparently, people with dentures do.

Lucy slid into her favorite PJs and climbed into her bed, sitting cross legged and giggling to herself as she sang "Criss Cross Applesauce spoons in a bowl" in her head. She then pulled the feedsack quilt up over her legs, the red and white pattern a lovely backdrop to the strange thimble-looking things, each fabric having its own texture. The trim was her favorite part. It was almost geometric with its red circles with small blue flowers in the center. Nestling into her bed, the blanket up to her nose, she pulled out the journal and thumbed back to where she had left off…

Riding in the brand-new Dodge and the farm truck in the same day is quite the contrasting experience.   Albert's dad's truck was not too old, but it had clearly been used on a farm, although I found the cleanliness of the interior surprising. Albert's dad said it was ok to call him "David" instead of "Mr. Trudeau," but I think it best to stay formal with my students' parents. He is very interesting -- he didn't talk at all about farming, but rather about his boys… all the way to my cousins house.

"So, do you like teaching?" David asked, as they pulled out of the driveway, the boys riding in the back of the truck.

"Yes, well, I haven't gotten to do much teaching *yet,* but when Laura has the baby, I'll step in more full time, " Grace shared, as she peaked through the back window at the two boys sitting with their backs pressed against the window. They were having fun laughing and carrying on.

"The boys enjoy you in class… Albert talks about you all the time and tells me you know a lot about music."

"Well, I don't know if I know a *lot,*" she said, smiling and looking over at her driver. The boys' dad had cleaned up quite a bit before jumping in the car, and his freshly starched shirt made him look like he was heading to church.   "My mother was a singer in New York, Grace continued. "She

A Ride Down the Road ©2019

performed every week -- many times -- and I was always with her. She sang all sorts of things. We would go to concerts and the symphony and plays. New York is quite different than here."

"Do you miss it?" he asked, glancing over at her. Their eyes met briefly, and he quickly turned back to look at the road.

Grace paused and sighed, looking out the window at the corn. It looked tall and crunchy.

"Sometimes, but I don't want to go back there. I like it here. I like the air, it's clean. And the people are friendly and not so hurried.   We sing at the house and Pastor plays his guitar, so there is music still. I miss the sea sometimes… the water there isn't much water here, though Pastor took us to the river last weekend. It was beautiful, the water and the hills. So clean, but also so cold! I loved it. Laura and I decided it was just as good as going to the beach," she laughed "Well, almost. Do *you* like it here? Are you from here?"

"Well, I live here now. My family is from Saint Louis, and many are still there… I have a sister who lives in the city. I don't like the city at all… and I assume that Saint Louis is much quieter than New York."

"Yes," Grace said, "The train stopped there, and the dowdiest businessman got on and sat in the seat next to me." Grace mimicked the man's movement and giggled, "I would suppose people from Saint Louis are not as friendly as here."

"No, they are not. It's just different," David replied. "Saint Louis is more like a city in the Northeast. My family… well… they own a business and keep a different pace. Here, I can take the boys to the river on the weekend -- we pack a lunch and just drive down for a Saturday and Sunday to go fishing."

"You should be coming to church," Grace blurted out, then realized she had been too direct. "I never see you there…

A Ride Down the Road ©2019

and it would be nice to see you and the boys… I mean, I don't mean to be rude."

She blushed awkwardly, then looked over to see if he was irritated. He glanced at her as he drove and smiled.

"It's ok, you are right. I should be bringing the boys to church. But after Rachel left… it's not that I don't believe or anything… but people talk. Even in church, *especially* in church. A single man with two kids… I guess I also just don't want to deal with it either. Everyone has an opinion, and no one ever asks what the truth is… sorry, that was probably too much." His voice faltered as he tried to justify his absence.

Grace felt awful, as if she had opened some wound. Instinctively, she reached over and touched his arm. "I am sorry. I didn't mean to bring up something painful." He glanced down at her hand.

Realizing her audacity in reaching out to touch him, she quickly drew her hand back.

"It's ok," David said, seeing her distress and trying to put her at ease. "It's been several years and she's moved on. She's remarried and only claims *that* family now. She didn't really want much to do with us. This wasn't exactly the life she had planned. She had ideas based on my family and well, a farm and this area just wasn't what she had in mind."
   He didn't look over as he talked just ran his hands nervously along the edges of the steering wheel. "The hardest part is the boys. Albert does not remember much but Ben does… he does not understand why she is gone and why she does not want to be his mom."

"So she just stays away? No communication with them… no connection?" Grace asked, as they pulled into the driveway at her cousin's home. David put the truck in park, then sat and stared at the steering wheel.

"I am not sure why, but she does not want to see the boys," he replied sadly. "They are better off this way. I know that sounds harsh." He stopped himself. They both looked at each other. Grace wanted to comfort him but was not sure what to say. They were startled out of the moment when they heard the boys thundering up to the house.

"Ms. Laura, are you there?!" Ben called, as he flung open the front door.

"I should go," Grace said, opening the car door and letting herself out. . David scrambled to get out of the truck and walk up the walkway behind her to retrieve the boys. They were met on the porch by Christopher, who had one boy tucked under each arm.

"David! My friend, come in and have some dinner!" the pastor said, looking like a pack mule. David smiled and patted his friend's shoulder.

"Wait, I have something for you." David hurried back to the truck and retrieved a basket of berries. "Blackberries are plentiful right now," he said as he walked up to the door.

"Well, I am sure Laura can make us something wonderful with these! Boys, come in and tell me about your adventures!" Pastor was always looking for an excuse to mingle with them.

He ushered them all inside, where Laura was setting out the meal.

"Oh!" she said. "I thought I might see you all tonight! Better yet, I see you come bearing gifts! Let me see about making us a pie tomorrow. Christopher, put those boys down before you break something."

He obliged and set the boys down who ran to their chairs followed by the adults. Laura and Christopher were at either end, the boys on one side, and David next to Grace on the other. Christopher laid his hand open on either side, David taking one and Ben taking the other. David opened his hand to Grace, and she lightly laid her hand in his. His hands felt rough from the field work and dark from all of the sun.   She thought her delicate fingers looked like a child's hand in his. She stared at them during the prayer and didn't notice when it ended. Luckily, David gave a light squeeze and she quickly looked up from the prayer and began to eat.

The conversation was lively as Ben regaled the group with the story of the newborn calf: How it was kind of gross and kind of exciting all at the same time. Albert seemed a little lost but joyfully ate his roll and dinner.

"Did you name it?" Grace asked, the chatter stopping briefly as everyone looked over at her.

"Name it?" asked David, glancing over at her. "Why would you name a cow?"

"Well, because it's a living thing and it's…I don't know really…" She laughed, realizing that farmers probably don't name things they are going to eat later.

"Well, we *could* name it…" said David, reluctantly. Ben chimed in, "How about Howard?"

"Isn't it a girl?" Albert asked, confused. "The mom is a girl…"

"Well, *you* are a boy and *your* mom is a girl," Ben said, rolling his eyes at his naive little brother. "It's a boy cow… I checked… it will fit in with our boy house."

Grace giggled -- she didn't know the topic of a name would be so entertaining. "Could you pass me the butter?" David asked quietly, not wanting to interrupt the boys fun.Grace smiled and passed it, their hands briefly touching in the exchange. Every time their eyes met, her heart raced a bit.

The boys jabbered and talked through the ideas of a name, then finally settled on "Stewart".

After dinner, the boys went outside to climb and play in the yard, and the men went out to the porch to talk. Laura and Grace headed to the kitchen to clean up.

"He is really a wonderful man," Laura said, looking out the window at David and her husband

"Who? Pastor?" Grace smiled and dried the dishes she was handed.

"No silly… David. He is a wonderful person and would be a smart match for you."

Grace stopped, her eyes wide. "Is *that* why you had me walk Albert home? So I could get a smart match?!" Grace laughed. "He is quite a bit older than me… what, 10 years? He is nice, but I don't know – why would his wife leave him? What did he do or not do?"

Laura stopped and almost dropped the dish. "He did nothing… that woman packed up and left him and those boys with just a letter about how she wanted more for her life then dirt and cows. She wanted to go back to Saint Louis and thought he should have used his education to better her situation. Grace, she left him because she wanted a lifestyle. She wanted what he had in Saint Louis: society, money, and status. She never had "enough" and she never was satisfied. She was never faithful, either… no matter what he believes or says… everyone knew she was not, but he felt called to stay."

Grace listened intently as Laura described the flawed marriage. It was a hopeless story where, in the end, David ended up alone for the last 5 years, raising the boys on his own. His wife left and sent him papers – even papers releasing the boys to him as if she never existed. Laura described the devastation and how Pastor had reached out and helped him.

"That's why he is always here helping… he says Pastor always cared for him even when he was in the pit at his

A Ride Down the Road ©2019

lowest, and that he will always care for Pastor. Even though he knows Christopher did it with no strings attached. They have a special bond, those two."

As the women finished the dishes, Grace decided to tell Laura about James Carter.

"Oh Laura - it was so embarrassing, but exciting too. He had the finest car I have ever seen, and his suit was certainly from New York," Grace stated, recounting the day's events to her cousin.

"He even told me I was beautiful!" Grace exclaimed.

"He said what?!" Laura replied concerned "But he just met you."

"I know," Grace replied "I don't think he meant to say it -- seemed to just slip out. But you know he must *think* it if he said it like that. AND he wants to visit tomorrow."

"Be careful, dear one," said Laura. "I understand this is exciting but remember to be wise. A man like James Carter comes from society… he lives a different life than we do… he may indeed think you are beautiful, but we live in different worlds. Remember to be wise. Those who ask for wisdom receive wisdom."

Grace could always count on her friend to share a scripture with every conversation. She sighed and continued to dry the dishes. Outside the window, she saw the two men sitting on the porch, chatting and laughing. The boys were playing and chasing each other in the yard, and it all just seemed so normal, so peaceful.

A Ride Down the Road ©2019

~ Chapter 5 ~

Seven days… Lucy quit counting all the deliciousness she was eating and asked her grandma for an apple. *Maybe that was her grandma's ploy the whole time, stuffing her so full that she'd not want to eat too much.*

"Grandma, is the man in the picture James Carter?" Her grandma seemed surprised to hear the name, and it made her bristle a bit as irritation briefly flashed across her face.

"No, dear…it's not." Lucy dug through the letter and found one from James Carter to Grace…it was a love letter, filled with niceties and flatteries.

"I don't get it! He wrote her stuff like *this*!" Lucy said, reading the letter aloud.

"Dear Grace,

Its difficult to be so far apart. I think of you often: How you smile at me and say my name. The way you laugh at my abhorrently unfunny jokes…"

"That's enough dear… I am the one who kept those letters… I know what they all say… I don't enjoy them." Grandma's voice was short but soft as she observed her granddaughter's surprised reaction. "Why did you keep them, then?" Lucy asked, still looking at the letter. She was rubbing the edges lightly. His handwriting was curly like Grace's. Maybe that was just a sign of the time, that people wrote beautifully, even the men. The letter was on bank letterhead.

"What happened to him? Did he die in the war? Did he die in a car crash?" Lucy realized how morose she sounded, but it was so intriguing, like a novel. She wished someone would write to *her* that way. The only explanation as to why Grace didn't run away with him and marry him is that he must have died. "If someone said those kinds of things about me, I would marry him." She clasped the letter to her

A Ride Down the Road ©2019

chest and sat back in the chair. As she did, she saw her Grandmas face looking troubled and disapproving. The lines of joy almost seemed darker, her face revealing tender memories of hurt and pain, mixed with a hint of anger.

"Would you, now?" her grandma said slowly, sighing heavily. "Even the devil has sweet words, my girl… maybe you should keep reading the journal I gave you… Don't be too wrapped up in his words. James was handsome and rich. He said all the right things to her and seemed to be a very smart match."

Lucy looked at the letter again. The paper had yellowed at the edges and had a texture to it different from the slick, crisp paper she had in her printer at home. It felt like thin fabric, or old newspaper that had softened over time.

"Lucy," her grandma started, "James Carter was a man wanting a beautiful wife on his arm to serve his purpose. He wanted her to make him look good to all of his friends and community. Grace was beautiful, but she was not confident in who she was as a child of God. This lack of confidence led to some difficult situations in her life. God's plan and God's timing are difficult to understand. When you are not confident in who you are in Him… well, it makes it challenging. Do you understand?"

Lucy nodded, looking back at the picture of Grace and the man.

"She weathered them all. Lucy, dear, God always gives us more than we can handle so that we know our position in this world. His sovereignty and His power are easier to learn when we are under strain. Sometimes, if we just see what others have been through, we can learn. Other times, we have to live through it. Grace was the 'live through it' type. She was strong-willed and smart. That got her through the loss of her mother and father. But sometimes, strength and beauty with a lack of confidence in God's plan… well it leads to challenges… .like your parents. They are both good,

A Ride Down the Road ©2019

intelligent people, but their lack of confidence in the plan God has for them is destroying them both."

Lucy felt her face redden as she thought about her parents. Grandma's voice trailed off a bit as she finished. "James Carter was confident in only himself… and only focused on his future."

Lucy was puzzled. From the letters he wrote, it seemed like James loved Grace, but clearly she was missing something.

"I am tired, dear. I need to go to bed," Grandma said, getting up to walk to her room. "Grandma," Lucy said, "It's still early. I'm going to go sit out on the porch."

She nodded, as if her words were gone for the evening. Lucy could tell that Grandma's heart seemed heavy. Reflecting on all that her grandma had shared with her, Lucy went to the swing with the journal and letters, hoping to get some clarity on Grandma's strange reactions to James.

James came to call on me. It's like a dream, really! He is so amazing and told me how much he enjoyed meeting me that it must have been fate that brought us together that day…

James stepped out of the car and walked up the path to the house. The parsonage was a dark red brick gothic revival with three sharply formed gables in front. It had a small square front porch and four posts holding up a small faux balcony with geometric and angled trim. The posts and balcony where white with green and black trim that matched the black shutters. The front walk was made of old bricks imprinted with the name of their manufacturer, the Independence Brick Company of Kansas. They had been salvaged from a building that had burned down in town years ago and had been carefully laid by church members from the driveway to the porch. Grace,hair in a messy low bun and flour on her face, answered the knock at the door. Still wearing her apron, she was expecting to see the familiar face of a church member. Her eyes grew large as she realized that it was James Carter, him in his perfect suit and

A Ride Down the Road ©2019

tie and her in a dirty apron with flour on her face. She was horrified.

"Oh, my!" she exclaimed, wiping her hands on her apron. "I, uh..."

"Grace," he said, looking somewhat delighted that he had caught her off guard, "James Carter... we met the other day, and..."

"Oh, yes, please come in," she said, stumbling backwards a bit but catching balance on the stair rail. Grace never could quite keep her feet underneath herself.

James stepped in the door and removed his hat, revealing a well-groomed head of wavy, dark hair. He quickly ran his hand through it to make sure it was in place and straightened his glasses. "I wanted to invite you to join me for dinner this evening. We would have to drive to Linchpin, but there is a lovely little café there that makes delicious food."

"Grace?" Christopher called, walking into the entryway with a smile on his face. Seeing James standing there seemed to take him by surprise. "Oh, hello. I'm sorry. I didn't realize someone was here. I'm Christopher, and you are?" he asked, stepping protectively in front of Grace.

James seemed confused at first and quickly shook Christopher's hand. "James Carter, I came to call on Grace, but I, uh...didn't... uh..." James stammered as he turned red and stepped back towards the door. Grace realized that, once again, he had mistaken her as taken.

"Christopher is my cousin." Grace said quickly and stepped forward next to him. "I live with Christopher and Laura here in this house. He is the pastor of the church in town, quite a lovely church. This is their home, and I live here with them," she said, reassuring her suitor of her current situation.

James was relieved, then realized he was still holding onto Christopher's hand.

"Oh, good, I mean, that's nice…wonderful, really…yes, that is a lovely church… nice to meet you," he stammered, quickly letting go and taking hold of his hat with both hands.

"Please come in and have a seat. Can we get you a lemonade or something? Sorry for the confusion," he said, as genuinely as he could. Christopher then ushered James into the parlor. "Grace, would you get us a lemonade for Mr. Carter?" He nodded towards the kitchen and smiled.

Grace hurried to the kitchen, where Laura was rolling out pie crust.

"Grace, where did you run off too?! We need to finish making the blackberry pie," Laura said, briefly looking up in time to see Grace taking off her apron and trying to use a spoon to see her reflection. "What are you doing?!" she laughed, amused by her obviously flustered friend. "Shhh!!!!" Grace said, looking panicked. "James Carter… James Carter came to the house and is here… he is in the parlor with Christopher. And oh, my… look at me! What do I do?! Oh, my!" Grace started to giggle and so did Laura. Grace frantically fixed her hair and pinched her cheeks to add color.

"Sweet girl," Laura said, wiping her hands on her apron, "Calm down! He is just a man, like any other man you meet at church or in town. Just a man!" Laura smiled as she took Grace's shaking hands. Laura used the edge of her apron to wipe the flour from her cousin's face.

But it was too late, Grace was completely swept up in the idea of James Carter and every handsome gaze he had sent her way. She quickly pulled four jelly jar glasses out of the cabinet and went to the fridge for the lemonade. As she poured, she found herself wishing she had some of the beautiful new glasses from Garret's store, he ones with the red, white and blue stripes that looked like summer. New

A Ride Down the Road ©2019

glasses were a luxury they could not afford. "No matter," she thought. "I am sure he wouldn't even notice that these are just recycled jelly jars."

She loaded the four glasses on a tray and walked into the parlor where Christopher and James were sitting. As she did, James stood quickly to his feet. No man had ever stood up for her when she entered a room.

She set the tray on the table and handed a glass to James. His hand brushed against hers lightly, like one would touch a delicate family heirloom, as the glass went from her to him. It made her melt a little inside and she smiled. Their eyes met briefly, and she was enamored with the depth of his dark eyes. His smile was perfect and suited him. She quickly sat down in the chair next to Christopher, who picked up his glass of lemonade.

"James, what brings you to Radical, Missouri." Christopher asked, taking a sip. The town had the most peculiar name. It was named for the "Radical Republicans" who settled the area as a campground to cross the White River. Ironically, it was not really that radical of a place at all, which is probably why it always elicited a reaction from visitors, either of amusement or surprise. In fact, "Radical, Missouri" seemed to be quite the oxymoron since the town only had a small general store, church, barber, post office, and really not much else. There was rumor of a gas station going in soon but that was mostly just a rumor.

"I am here on business. I had reason to stop and visit one of the farmers in town. We own the mortgage at the bank. We needed to…" he paused a bit, choosing his words carefully, "…have a discussion. I often make those visits myself to make sure that everything is communicated well. It's a great responsibility to lead an entire bank."

"Indeed." Christopher replied. Grace caught the brief eyebrow movement that indicated something was said that he was not pleased about. "And will you be staying, or heading back to Springfield?"

A Ride Down the Road ©2019

"Well, I was coming by to see if Grace would want to join me for dinner tonight. I found this great place up the road in Linchpin." Again, Grace caught the slightest look of disapproval on her cousin's face. Grace knew that Christopher felt he had taken on the role of both cousin and parent since she arrived. She was sure that he didn't approve of a man asking her to dinner without asking him first, and certainly not of taking her as far as Linchpin alone.

"We wouldn't hear of it." Christopher said, then paused for a moment as a partial smile crept from the edge of his mouth. "I mean, you must stay for dinner with us. We would love to have you and would enjoy the opportunity to get to know you better."

James was a bit surprised, and he was not sure he wanted to stay for dinner. It was clear that he was seeking time with Grace, but also clear that this wasn't just an invitation, it was the only way he was having dinner with her.

"Well, that's very generous of you, but I hate to impose, and…" James sputtered. Christopher quickly interrupted, "No imposition at all, not at all! And my wife, Laura, is the best cook in town. Right now, she's in the middle of making a blackberry pie. It's the most incredible thing you will ever taste!"

James smiled and nodded. "Thank you, that is very kind. I can't say no to blackberry pie. I'll gladly stay!

The meal was humble but delicious: Meatloaf, mashed potatoes, green beans, and homemade rolls. Laura was well-known for her baking. The foursome ate, and James shared about the bank, Springfield, and his travels. Grace asked questions and listened like a child listens to someone reading them a story.

"Laura, that was delicious. I must say it is far better than the café in Linchpin." James said, as he dabbed his mouth with his napkin. "I appreciate the invitation."

"I am glad you enjoyed it, Mr. Carter," said Laura, as she stood up to collect the empty plates. Grace quickly followed her lead and started to take things to the kitchen.

As soon as the ladies left the room, James looked across the table at the pastor.

"Pastor, you really are a lucky man, your wife is an amazing cook. Grace is very lucky to have such a great teacher. I was quite taken with her the other day when I saw her walking that boy home. Quite lucky that I was driving that road that day. Quite lucky indeed."

"Luck is an interesting term, you know," Christopher said, as he looked across the table at his guest.

"Oh, I know… I know," James interrupted, "'Blessed' would probably be the right term for *you*. Do you not believe in luck?"

"Luck? No, I don't believe in luck or fate or happenstance or anything like that, but rather in divine intervention and God's plan."

"You believe that everything happens for a reason that there is a time for everything and a reason," James said, with a chuckle. "Don't get me wrong, Pastor. I believe in the Almighty but I also believe that He can't possibly know everything that will happen. Fate and luck must still exist in some capacity it's not all blessing or curse."

"Your Almighty does not sound very 'Almighty' at all if He is unaware that you would be driving down a road that day," Christopher replied dryly with a smile.

The girls walked back in each carrying two pieces of pie on plates. The plates were Laura's mothers, and there were only 6 of them total in the whole set. They were white with 3 blue flowers around the edges. "Flow blue" is what they were called because the design had blurred edges as if the pattern bleed when it was originally put on and glazed. The flowers were edged with gold-painted swirls. Grace loved them because they made her think of their early years growing up together.

The blackberry juice ran out of the edge of the pie and the crust seemed to absorb it like a sponge. The top of each piece of pie had a carefully cut leaf and was sprinkled with sugar that crystalized on top during the baking against the golden-brown flakiness. It looked like heaven on a plate with a dollop of homemade whipped cream on the side.

James smiled as the plate was placed in front of him. He loaded his spoon with a bite of pie and cream then took a bite. "Oh, my, Laura, this is delicious! It's like nothing I have ever tasted before in my life. Delicious! I know this is better than that café! Forget ever going *there* if you can have food like this *here*," James said, as he avoided the continued conversation with the pastor. "Laura, do you cook and prepare all day for your husband?"

Laura laughed and smiled. "No, no I am the teacher at the school, but Grace will be taking over for me soon. She is going to become the new schoolteacher after our little one arrives," Laura said, rubbing her belly lightly

"Really?" James said, looking at Grace, who was lifting a bite of pie to her mouth. "Do you *want* to work?"

"Well," Grace said, quickly lowering her precious bite back to the plate. "I um… well, I enjoy the children and teaching them. Each day, they are getting to know me and I them. They are each so special."

"Grace has been a great blessing to us," Christopher said, reaching over and squeezing her hand. "We love having her here."

The conversation continued as they finished their pie. James spoke a lot of Springfield and how exciting things were there now and of his work at the bank.

"Grace, would you my going for a stroll with me while it's still light outside?" James asked, looking directly at Grace, and avoiding eye contact with Christopher. Grace looked over at Christopher for approval. He nodded in agreement and she stood to leave.

"But don't go far, I don't want you to be out too late. We have school tomorrow," Laura said, clearing off the table. Grace began to pick up plates. "I can get these, sweet one," Laura said. "Go on." Grace smiled and nodded, so excited that she could hardly contain herself.

James grabbed his hat and placed it on his head as he opened the door for Grace. As soon as the door closed behind them, he offered her his arm. She gladly slipped her hand in the nook of his elbow crease. They walked across the yard and down the dirt road towards the school.

"Tell me, why do you live with your cousins?" James asked, observing the land around them and then looking at his walking partner. "Where are your parents?"

"My father left long ago. I believe he died, but I don't know. And my mother... she was killed in a fire." Grace replied.

"I am so sorry to hear that," he said, placing his hand on top of hers. "So you're all alone?"

"Not exactly. I have Christopher and Laura, and the town. And the church members, who are quite fond of me. It seems as though they have all adopted me. They are sending me to college in January to go to get my teaching certificate. I am going to fill-in for Laura for a few months while she gets settled with the baby then I going to college. Can you believe it? Me? With my own teaching certificate!" Grace almost skipped as she told him.

"College?" he smiled, admiring her youthful spirit. "That would be quite an accomplishment." Grace agreed and asked him about his college experience. James shared several stories about college life and his college friends.

How they went to football games and are now all lawyers and doctors. All had become pillars of their communities, just like him. Soon they arrived at the school, and Grace opened the door to show him the classroom.

"One classroom?" he asked. "I didn't realize that one-room schoolhouses still existed."

"We don't go through high school, only through the 6th grade. Then, the kids who want to continue on go to the high school in Branson."

"That seems far," he said, walking to the window and looking out towards the town. "It really is a small town, not much here. But maybe when the lake is built, it will help it."

"What lake?"

"The Corps of Engineers is going to flood the lowlands and make a lake for visitors for camping and boats. It will be quite a feet!" James replied, his hands motioning the vastness of the coming lake.

"What will that mean for the farmers in the lowlands? I mean all of those that are on higher lands should be fine, but what about the lowlands?" Grace asked, concerned for her students and their families.

James shrugged. "I am not sure. I just know the Corps of Engineers is going to build a lake, and it will bring a lot of travelers to the land. It will help bring money to the region maybe even fund a high school in this area so the kids don't have to travel so far."

"But where will they go?" Grace asked, looking out the window of the school. It sat in the highland area, but she could see through the old windows the valleys that might flood.

"Well, right now, they already have to deal with the constant flooding. It is really for their best interest. The government will buy their land and they can buy something new." James hesitated, then changed the subject. "So, will you be going to Springfield for school?" he asked, then continued without waiting for her answer, "That would be a pleasant thing for me. I would enjoy seeing you more often."

"I would enjoy that, too," she said with a smile, then walked back to where he was standing. He offered his arm again. "The sun is starting to set, we should go back to the house," he said softly, and the two walked back to the house. The sky was pink and purple like a watercolor painting. The perfect setting for their romantic stroll.

Walking her to the front porch, James turned to Grace. "I had a wonderful time with you tonight. Would it be okay with you if we wrote to one another? And then if I came to call again the next time, I'm in town?"

"Of course," Grace said with a nervous smile, looking down at her feet.

James started to touch her cheek lightly, but the door opened slowly, revealing Christopher standing there in the dim light. He cleared his throat.

"Well," James said, quickly dropping his hand to his side, "I will write. Thank you for a lovely stroll. Pastor, please thank your wife again for her hospitality."

James walked quickly to his car and drove away. Grace watched until she could only see dust coming up from behind the car. Then Grace turned to her cousin and gave him an enthusiastic hug. "Oh, my word! He is wonderful!" she exclaimed.

~ Chapter 6 ~

Day 8, Lucy and Grandma decided to drive to town for some shopping in Grandma's old gray Buick. Grandma had two extra cushions on her side that she sat on to help her see over the steering wheel. The interior was clean and otherwise respectable, but Lucy giggled at the tape deck. The radio was set to the oldies station and Grandma sang along with every song. As they drove to town, Lucy looked out the window and admired the scenery. It didn't seem so overwhelming anymore, nor did the cows seem to be living such a miserable existence as they did when she first arrived. The fields swayed with the wind and made her think of Grace's journal. She tried to picture the sea in the same way as they waved. But Lucy had only seen the ocean once, so it just looked like wheat to her.

"Grandma, where is the parsonage? Is it close?" She asked, as they turned off the long dirt driveway to the black top.

"It's a bit outside of town, dear. We can drive by, but it's in disrepair now. No one has lived there since, well, for years," she replied.

The song changed to Stevie Nicks' "Landslide", and Grandma smiled as she turned up the volume.

"I took my love and took it down ...climbed the mountain and turned around ...saw my reflection in a snow covered hill and the landslide brought me down," Grandma sang as loud as she could. She looked over at Lucy. "You know, you can stay as long as you want dear… all summer, even. I have enjoyed you here."

Lucy smiled. It felt good to be wanted, and she knew that the love her grandma had for her was something that didn't need to be earned. Her grandma would do anything for her. She knew that her parents "loved" her, too, but right now, she felt like she was just getting in their way. All of their arguing about *their happiness* seemed so hollow like *she* wasn't even a part of the picture.

A Ride Down the Road ©2019

She recalled conversations from the drive to Grandma's, mother confessing to feeling trapped and wanting more freedom for her life. Lucy felt like she was creating these stories in her head about her unhappiness. Her dad was never verbally or physically mean maybe distant and stuck in his own head, but not intentionally. He had always been that way, too smart for his own good and not focused on anything but his work. Regardless, they both seemed so focused on their *own* needs that *her* life didn't matter, and it was only about their happiness. In every phone call, they focused on their inability to stay together, with some mention of the frustrating struggles in their marriage. Her mom described "how it was so hard to get along". The more they called and complained, the more she felt her heart freezing and hardening. It made the journals and letters even more attractive.

"Now I've been afraid of changing because I built my life around you. But time makes you bolder, children get older… I'm getting older, too." Grandma sighed as she sang the "I am getting older…" line.

Knowing logically that the potential dissolution of her parents' marriage was not her fault yet *feeling* it in her heart was hard. Being wanted was a balm to her soul. Her grandma had told her daily how much her Father in heaven loves her and desires a relationship with her. Lucy had tried to understand that but having someone demonstrate that unconditional love was helpful. Maybe the changes wouldn't be too bad.

As they drove into town, Lucy admired the aged buildings. The town was made up of a downtown square with a large courthouse in the middle and bright green manicured grass at each corner. The buildings were different types of brick but all two stories, connected in a row on all four sides. Some of the buildings had hand-carved stone cornice edging the top like frosting on a cake. The lower levels housed stores with large windows that banked the side of the doors, some flat and some with angular bays filled with goods. They pulled onto the square and parked in front of the small grocery store on the corner. Across the street, at an angle,

A Ride Down the Road ©2019

was a True Value Hardware, and its window was filled with flags and a grill. The "open" sign was illuminated.

Grandma parked the car and gave Lucy some cash. She told her to use it if she needed a Coke. Lucy watched as she got out of the car and walked across the street to the beauty shop. Lucy followed behind her but stopped in front of a cute antique shop with a large bay window. The large window was set with a 4th of July display. Blue and white dishes hung on the wall in a wispy pattern as if a large gust had blown them and they were stuck to the wall. There was a red antiqued drop-leaf table set for a party, small bits of white paint showing through the worn edges. Blue and white cloth napkins were the place mats for stacks of yellow fiesta ware dishes. An inviting glass pitcher with red, white, and blue pinstriped rings around it and matching glasses were displayed at each seat.

Lucy lost herself in the display until a loud truck pulled in behind her. It was green and old with rounded wheel wells and wood edges on the bed. The bed of the truck was filled with antiques. A lanky guy wearing a sleeveless Nike shirt and a Cardinals baseball ball cap jumped out.   He glanced over at Lucy and smiled a wide, toothy grin, then dove in to his work of emptying the bed. A woman came hurrying out of the shop and she gave him a quick hug as they started to unload the antiques. There was a dresser with carved, acorn handles that had been painted gray on the bottom, the wooden top stained dark. It had small boxes on the top and looked as if, at one point, it might have housed a mirror.

The boy looked back at Lucy as he carried the dresser and smiled. Lucy felt uncomfortable and blushed, trying to figure out where to go. He was handsome... but was wearing a Cardinals hat. "Not sure we could be friends," she giggled to herself.

Lucy crossed the street and walked towards the large gazebo there in the park. Plopping herself down on a park bench, she pulled the journal and letters from her drawstring knapsack. The rumble of a truck engine made her glance up. The green truck from the antique shop passed by and the driver waved. She still couldn't get over the hat, but smiled and went back to her reading.

We went to the river today for a full day of fun. I had to ride in the jump seat… not my favorite thing, but at least we got there. I must say the Nash is not that practical, but it's better than the wagon, I suppose. It cuts the ride in half.

Grace climbed out of the car. She had paired a three-quarter sleeve gingham shirt with a nice pair of pants that she had received from one of the ladies at church. She felt stylish, like something out of a magazine. She helped Laura with the picnic basket, and they found a flat spot in the grass close to the rocky edge of the river. Laura laid out a patchwork quilt made of feed sacks that she pieced last year. It had multiple colors in the different patterns and a yellow edge.

"Grace, how are you?" Laura asked, as she carefully sat down next to the basket. Her round belly made it difficult to maneuver.

"How am I doing?" Grace replied, laughing. "I am ok." She knelt by the basket and began to pull out the food.

"Grace, you've had so many changes, what with your mom, and then moving here," Laura said, helping her unwrap the food. Grace busied herself with picnic prep until Laura grabbed her hand. "Its ok, you know, to talk about it all."

Grace took a deep breath and looked up from her work. "Some days, I think I am good and not going to cry about her being gone… but I always seem to find a way to see something, hear something, or smell something that reminds me of her. Then I miss her."

Laura squeezed her hand. "I know -" Laura started, but was interrupted when Christopher walked up with his fishing pole in hand.

"Well, ladies, that looks delicious!" he said, reaching for an apple slice, "I am not sure where David is. He said that he would be here by noon."

"It's not like him to be late," Laura said. "He'll be here soon enough."

"I am sure he will be here shortly - he does not like to miss fishing," laughed Christopher. He grabbed another apple slice, then walked to the water's edge to start his hunt.

"Laura, I really appreciate yours and Christopher's generosity. For letting me stay here and for getting me a job," Grace said, watching Christopher cast his line into the river. The air smelled of fall and fresh water. The water was edged with a mixture of tall pine trees and proud oaks, casting their shadows over their sitting area.

"When will you believe me when I say we are family, and this is just what family does for one another!" Laura said, smiling as Grace leaned back on the blanket. She laid her head on the blanket next to Laura's belly.

"I do believe you," Grace replied, melting into the blanket as Laura played with her dark hair. Grace stared at the clouds. She and her mother would go to the park weekly and watch the clouds. They took turns describing the shapes and admiring God's artwork. "Each one unique," her mother would sing. "Each one its own special design. Just like you and just like me." Even the clouds made her remember.

"Laura, when did you know that Christopher was the one for you? When were you *sure*?" Grace asked, watching the clouds floating in the sky.

"Well, we were friends - good friends. We helped at the church together many times. That was really the only time we were able to see one another at first. He worked with his father most days," Laura replied, as she watched her husband pull in a fish from the water and hold it up like a trophy. She clapped and blew him a kiss. "It was at a revival when I *knew*... I listened to him as he spoke to a man. The man had lost everything - his family, his home, his money - he had nothing left. It was all his own undoing and bad choices that caused his downfall. Christopher spoke to him with such love and compassion. Treated him as an equal... treated him with respect as he explained the gospel.

A Ride Down the Road ©2019

I knew he was special, but it wasn't until that moment that I knew *how* special." Laura quickly grabbed Grace's hand and placed it on her stomach. She could feel the baby kick against her hand with little thumps. They both giggled as Grace sat up and put both hands on her stomach to feel the pulse.

"And it didn't hurt that he was handsome… I remember your letters at that time," Grace laughed, letting go of her friend and hugging her knees to her chest.

"Yes," Laura laughed. "He is handsome, but, more than that, he is kind, genuine, and always helps me love God more. That's what I hope for you sweet cousin… and that he is handsome."

They laughed as the green truck pulled up and the boys jumped from the back, running to Christopher with their poles. David followed, calling to the boys as he grabbed the creel basket and pail.

"Hello, ladies!" he yelled, raising his poles to wave. David set things down to shake hands with Christopher. They laughed and chatted as David prepared his pole and cast a hook into the water. The boys found a spot and sat together fishing. Grace smiled at the scene. It looked like something out of a magazine advertising vacations, not something as simple as real life.

"Sometimes, this all does not feel real," she said, staring at the scene, trying to sear it into her memory.

"What… fishing and having a picnic?" Laura asked.

"All of it… I mean, it's like something out of a magazine, not something real. It's like when I would visit you at the sea. It always seemed like a picture, not real life." Grace said, picking up a twig and using it as a pencil on the ground. "I couldn't imagine this."

"It's real, and it's your life and we are your family," Laura said matter-of-factly, smiling and rubbing the sides of her stomach "This is *all* real."

A Ride Down the Road ©2019

"I just can't get over the idea that this is normal," Grace said. David pulled his first fish from the water. It was large and the men cheered. They held it up for their fan club on the blanket, and they obliged with cheers and laughter.

"The eating will be good tonight!" David hollered from the shoreline, as he stood and bowed. "It will be a glorious fish fry!" They all laughed at the theatrics.

Grace soaked it all in. As the day went on, the men finished fishing and sat down for lunch. The crew laughed and talked. It seemed like the perfect day, just like Grace said: like something out of a magazine.

~ Chapter 7 ~

Lucy finished reading and decided to go explore the antique shop since the truck was gone. There was a bell hanging above the door that rang as she entered.

"Welcome! Let me know if you need anything," called a voice from a room behind the cashier's desk.

"Ok, thanks!" Lucy replied making her way down the aisles. Each booth was unique with its own theme or collection. She found herself in a large booth with a bicycle hanging from the ceiling. It was a vintage green color and had a basket filled with flowers. The booth was filled with antique painted furniture. A large green buffet had a display of ironstone and tea towels with brightly colored flowers. Lucy smiled as she examined the intricate design of the booth. It was clear each piece had been placed to create vignettes, but somehow it felt like it was telling a story as well.

"Do you like Irontsone?" The voice startled Lucy, and she whipped around quickly to find the brunette that helped unload the truck. "I am not familiar with it," replied Lucy.

The woman walked into the booth and picked up the white pitcher from the display, then showed it to her. "This is Ironstone - it's a Meakin from the 1890s called block optic. Some people like McCoy or Roseville, but, to me, the simple beauty of whiteware Ironstone is my favorite. Are you interested in antiques?"

"Me?" Lucy asked, not sure how to answer. "Well, I think they are nice. My grandma has several, but I don't think she sees them as special - just as her things. I am staying with her for a few weeks. Her name is Laura."

"Oh! Everyone knows Grandma, and she is *everyone's* Grandma. My boys are rather attached to her," she replied. The front doorbell rang and she turned to walk back up front. "Holler if you need anything! I am Kary, by the way."

"Do you mind if I find a place to sit for a bit while I wait for Grandma?" Lucy asked.

"Sure! Try booth 340 on the 2nd row, 3 booths in, on the right." Kary replied, as she rushed up front to greet the visitors.

Lucy wandered through the rest of the store and found the recommended spot. There was a large reupholstered Queen Ann chair. It was covered in blue-striped feed sack and painted in white chalk paint. The distressing was so good it looked as if it had aged that way.   She pulled a suitcase that had been converted into an ottoman up to her feet, pulled the stash of old letters out of her purse, and sat back to do some reading while she waited.

Many of the letters started out simply with "Dear Grace" or "Dear James" but they quickly progressed to more romantic terms. She loved seeing how the relationship progressed just by reading their notes to each other.

Dearest Grace,

My days at the bank seem long, and I come home to a large empty home. Nothing but my dog, whose name is Doug, and my cook. Doug is a small sheep dog with white and brown spots. One eye is blue and one is brown. I have had him for years. I would bring him along the next time I visit, but he is old and does not travel well. I think you would enjoy him very much.

Today at the bank I helped an older couple. They had been married 48 years and are delightful. The gentleman is named John and his wife is Loren. (Spelled just like that!) They were so in love and looking forward to the next trip to Chicago to see their grandson. Wouldn't grandchildren be wonderful – of course children come first but all of it sounds wonderful. This house not being empty and Doug with more friends to play with other than just me would be great.

How is the preacher and his wife? The school and kids? Did you hear more about the college idea? I know that you think this is a great idea. I am glad you will be close by for a while, but it is not necessary for you to work the rest of your life.   A woman should not need to work once she is married.

Yours,

James

Lucy found the response from Grace and giggled as she read. Nothing took her mind off of her situation more than the letters.

Dearest James,

I would quite like to meet Doug. He must certainly be a very nice companion. I am sure he enjoys every aspect of his lazy life at home.

The life we could have together is such a dream. A home and a family is everything I have ever dreamed of for my life. I can see it all in my head.

Christopher and Laura are good. She told me that she has taught me all she knows, and the town has agreed to pay for me to get a teaching certificate. I will be coming to Springfield! Isn't that wonderful? The kids are a little sad that I will be leaving in a month… especially Albert. He sits so close to me each day practically on my lap. He misses his mother, but she wants nothing to do with him. His father is a very kind and dutiful father, but a boy needs a mother just as much. I will miss him most of all.

I understand your feelings about working – we have talked before but I want to be able to use my certificate to serve the town. I like to teach and like my time there – it's very fulfilling.

I am very pleased to be more available to visit you. While I enjoy your visits, it will be good to be able to see you more often. I would like that very much.

Yours,

Grace

Lucy pulled out the journal and flipped through it, looking for the dates that corresponded to their written exchanges.

My mind is filled with James… I can't stop thinking about him. I am so pleased to be going to Springfield for a teaching certificate. It's only a few months to be away from here, but so much change for me. New York, Radical, and now there... I will have him to help me adjust. So much change, but I know it will be good… I feel God is in it (as Christopher would say) -- just not sure how to make it all work.

Grace stared out the window of the church as Christopher preached about God's sovereignty. Understanding that everything that happens builds who we are and why we are here to serve and support others.

The church sat on a clearing that overlooked the rolling Ozark mountains. The autumn trees looked like a watercolor painting through the window, with edges blending together. The reds, yellows, and oranges were bright in the morning sun.

"Psst…" She felt a tap on her shoulder. She turned to see Albert, his freckled face smiling at her as he passed a small piece of paper. His father cleared his throat and furled his brow at the boy. Grace looked over at him and smiled as she accepted the gift from the boy. David had become like one of their family, spending many Sunday lunches at their home and showing up to help Christopher with projects. Last week he showed up with a 1928 Nash with 4 doors. It was green with wood spoke wheels. He had bought it from another farmer during a delivery for $25. He and Christopher worked and worked to get it running. Then he spent the evening in the family room talking and sharing stories, laughing and joking. Christopher used it often to help people in town, even taking them clear to Springfield to see a doctor on occasion.

David smiled back as he resumed his focus on the sermon. Grace unfolded the paper and it revealed a small picture of a stick figure boy holding a flower handing it to a stick figure woman. She loved that boy.

Laura glanced over at her, grinning as she rubbed her belly and adjusted her position. The baby would certainly come soon. The changes were happening so fast: losing her mother, gaining her new family (soon to be expanding!), and now going off to college. In her wildest dreams she could have never imagined having the opportunity to go to college and get a teaching certificate. But somehow, all of the bad things had resulted in a redirection of her life to this moment. Maybe Christopher was on to something. As the sermon ended, the congregation rose and sang a closing hymn. Everyone filed out into the front entrance and stopped to greet Christopher and Laura. She looked so tired but stood dutifully next to her husband and shook hands with all the members passing by.

Albert grabbed Grace's hand and pulled her towards the parsonage. A small herd of children followed them. "Ms. Grace, can we play cowboys and robbers in your yard?"

Before she could answer, David stepped behind. "Albert, go and play with your friends. Ms. Grace does not want to do that and feed you, too." Albert released her hand and took off running.

"Thank you," she said, smiling at him. "How are the new puppies at the farm?"

"They are good, and all of them made it, fortunately. I thought for sure we would lose the small one, but he is pulling through. He seems to have a lot of will to survive. They will wean in a few weeks, and some of them will have to find new families. We can't keep all of them – though I think it might break Albert's heart," he said, looking over at the children as they ran and laughed in the yard.

"Well, new families aren't so bad. It has been good for me," Grace said, glancing at the children, then up at David's blue eyes. "I mean – before, it was just me and my mom. We had enough, though we were never rich. Now, look at all I have: a family, friends – I am rich!" She looked over at the children and reveled in their joy.

"Grace, I know that soon you will be leaving for school. I wanted to talk with you about –" he began to say, but was interrupted by a hand on his shoulder.

"Well, I am starved!" Christopher announced loudly, smiling at David and Grace. "Let's go eat!"

David looked discouraged, but said "Yes, Pastor let's break some bread." The men laughed and walked into the house. David turned back and smiled at her.

"What were you two talking about?" Laura asked, taking the hand of her sweet cousin

"I don't know… you know David and I just talk about things. Nothing and anything… today, it was the dog, and tomorrow, who knows… probably Albert's reading," Grace replied nonchalantly, as she and Laura walked to the house. Laura paused and grabbed the side of her stomach, squeezing Grace's hand as pain shot through her body.

"Oh, my!" she said, looking faint. Grace quickly grabbed her friend to support her.

"Laura, are you ok? What's wrong?!" Grace demanded.

"Well, this has been happening all morning… it may be time," gasped Laura, breathlessly.

"Albert!" Grace called, "Go get Pastor and your dad" Albert quickly left his friend and ran into the house. Within moments, Christopher flew out the door, David right behind him. He scooped his wife up in his arms and carried her into the house.

"Don't worry, love – it will be ok!" He hurried into the house. Grace, following close behind, stopped quickly and turned to David.

"David, I need you to go get the doctor," she said, standing on the step to the porch. In the excitement of the moment, she put both hands on his chest as fear and anticipation rushed through her body.

"Ok, I can do that," he said nervously, as she threw her arms around his neck and hugged him, slipping from the stairs into his arms. "It's time for our family to grow! I am so happy, " she said, laying her head against his chest.

A Ride Down the Road ©2019

"Me, too," he said, stumbling to find more words. Grace released him, then ran into the house. David stood watching her go, then hurried off to get the doctor.

After several hours had passed, a baby's cry was heard through the door all the way into the parlor. Moments later, Grace hurried into the room and both men stood up nervously.

"It's a boy!" she cried joyously, hugging Christopher. He stood in shock as she shook him a bit. "You can go in now – go on!" He quickly pushed past her and hurried into the room.

Exhausted, Grace flopped on the couch, and David joined her.

"A boy is good," he said, gazing earnestly at the small fire crackling in the fireplace. "Yes, it will be good for them to have one. I mean, if he's anything like *your* boys, he will be a joy," she replied softly, looking over at her friend. "David, what did you want to talk to me about earlier – is everything ok?"

He looked down at his hands, then hesitated. Grace could sense that something was wrong.

"David… what's wrong?" she asked, reaching over and touching his arm.

"Nothing, really it was nothing… I wanted to tell you how happy I was for you to get to go to school. How amazing it would be to get a certificate and how wonderful that would be for all of us in the town." He seemed to piece together words, his eyes searching her face intently. "I mean – it's amazing for you and such a great thing you will be able to do for the community. Clearly, you are gifted with teaching."

Grace smiled and settled back into the couch "So you don't think it's a bad idea? I mean, that I should go to college and teach?"

A Ride Down the Road ©2019

"What do you mean? It's an amazing opportunity, and besides, there is never harm in education – it's always beneficial."

"If I ever marry someday, then maybe I shouldn't work – I mean, teaching is…"

"What are you talking about?   You have always said that you love teaching and caring for the children. Marrying does not change that -- it simply adds a partner into your life."

Grace smiled. That was a good way to put it. She filed it away into her head for future conversations. The fire smoldered in front of them, and she closed her eyes to rest them but quickly drifted into sleep. David covered her with a quilt and slipped out the door.

~ Chapter 8 ~

Lucy heard the clock toll from courthouse in the middle of the square. She quickly repacked the letters and the journal, then walked to the front of the store to find Kary to say goodbye. Kary was preoccupied with measuring a large boxy wardrobe for some customers. It looked like something from the Civil War, with beautiful swirly wood on the sides and a large mirror in the middle.

"Thank you!" Lucy called, as she walked out the door.

"Come again -- anytime!" Kary replied quickly, then returned to her discussion on the size of the wardrobe.

The air was warm and moist, but the cool breeze made her walk in the sunshine tolerable. Each of the buildings that lined the street were unique, even though they shared a wall. One had an engraved stone header that read "Hardware and Furniture" with a large sun-shaped medallion above it dated 1897. The windows were rectangular with triangles on top, and the stone trim of the building was cut into diamond shapes with small circles inside. Instead of red bricks, the building was made of tan, square stones. It looked like it was once a bank, although now it housed a flower shop. She kept walking until she reached the end of the block and found the beauty shop tucked into the side of a building. The window was large and clean with the name "Josie" painted on it in large, curly letters. Inside, the pink tile floor was home for a row of chrome hair dryers one side and shiny white and silver styling chairs on the other. It was like stepping into the 1950s. Older ladies sat beneath the dryers with their magazines and Diet Cokes, waiting for their turn with a tall, wiry hairdresser named Josie. She was teasing and prepping Grandma's perfectly-formed gray curls to look like a helmet – just like she liked it.

"Hello, dear!" she called, as Lucy stood smiling at the scene. It reminded her of something between *Grease* and *Steel Magnolias*. "Come in and sit in one of the chairs. I'm almost done."

"Hi," said the waif-like hairdresser with a pixie haircut and a nose piercing. "I am Josie, we love your grandma! She is wonderful."

"Thanks," Lucy said, sitting in the chair next to Grandma "I like your tattoo. What does it mean?"

"Mean?" asked Josie, glancing at the sparrow inked onto her arm, then back at Lucy. She leaned over to show the bird more clearly to her new friend. "Well, friend… some may say 'freedom'– you know, 'fly high and free like a bird.' Others may say 'Seize the day.' But I say that it helps me remember that if God will care for even a sparrow, then He is going to take care of His own, which is all of us." With that, she went back to her work teasing and primping Grandma's hair.

A voice started singing from under a dryer across the room, "His eye is on..." the Spaaaarrrrooooow… and I know he watches…"

Then, out of nowhere, Josie chimed in, "Yes, I know He watches..."

The other voice picked it up again, hitting a beautiful high note, "And I know He watches…"

"Meeee," sang both voices together.

Lucy turned and saw an older woman who had shut off her dryer to make sure the song rang through the parlor. She was wearing a bright pink button down shirt and a khaki skirt.

"Gurl, we know He watches us. We know! We know! We know!" The sweet southern voice was accompanied by a face painted bright with makeup. "Some days, I just have to preach it to make myself believe it. I know! Know! KNOW!"

The ladies laughed and smiled with one another as the woman got up and walked towards Lucy.

A Ride Down the Road ©2019

"You must be Lucy. I understand you are why there is no fudge this week from Grandma!"

"Now, Val – I told you that we both indulge," Grandma said, looking very cross.

"Well, I look forward to that fudge and am wondering why you didn't help her make some more."

Lucy sat smiling, watching the entire circus of ladies chime in about fudge, cookies, cakes and whatever else Grandma seemed to bring to town each week for her hair adventure.

"You see, we don't have to fight Miss Josie – there is nothing to that little feather who might blow away. But the rest of us -- namely, me, because I really don't care what these other ladies need… mainly *me*, in my inability to bake anything without a black crusty edge of char -- need some delightful wonderments to make their way to the beauty shop!" Val proclaimed, wagging her finger at Grace.

At this point, Lucy could not tell if the woman who seemed to cast a shadow over her was being funny or serious as she replied, "Well, I… uh… I just you know…"

"I need to tell you something, girl," continued the woman.

"Now, Val – leave the poor sweet girl alone – she is taking care of me this summer, and I don't want you to scare off my companion," Grandma said, as she stood to her feet and walked over to her friend. She looked like Jack without a beanstalk next to the giant of a woman.

"I am just giving her trouble – I *would* like to have some fudge… but I know…" she began, with a wink at Josie, then broke into a Branson stage rendition of "His Eye is on the Sparrow." Lucy wasn't sure if the ladies under the dryers would join in, like a stage show, or if this was just for Val's entertainment. When she finished, the room erupted with clapping and laughter. "And of *that,* my friend, you can see

A Ride Down the Road ©2019

an encore presentation at church on Sunday!" Val said, as Grandma gave her a quick hug and kiss on the cheek.

"We will see you later." Grandma laughed.

Grandma and Lucy walked out the door and back onto the square. "Would you like a treat from the Casey's? I would love some pizza – it's my favorite – we could get one and take it home," Grandma said, giggling, as she took Lucy's hand and headed down the street to the car. No McDonalds, no Burger King nothing but a Casey's. "What could it hurt," said Lucy to herself, "Pizza would complement and enhance my diet of cookies, biscuits, and gravy."

As they entered the store, Lucy ran smack into a young man wearing a red vest. He had been carrying a box full of candy bars, but they were now scattered all over the floor.

"Oh, I am SO sorry!" Lucy exclaimed in horror, dropping to her knees and picking up as many as she could.

"It's ok -- things happen," he said, joining her as she scrambled to collect all the pieces.   "My name is Ethan. What's yours?" He asked.

"Lucy," she said, looking up into the sea blue eyes of her accidental assault victim. "I am here with my grandma."

"Ethan! What are you doing down there?" Grandma's voice said loudly, trying to compensate for the music blaring from behind the cash register. "I dropped them," he said, smiling at Lucy. Then, hopping to his feet, he quickly went and leaned his head down so Grandma could kiss the top. He wasn't much taller than her, and his sandy blond hair was sunkissed with natural blonde highlights.   She gently grabbed his freckled cheeks with her thin hands. "How are you, my wonderful friend?" she asked.

"Good...except for the candy incident here with this new girl." Ethan stared at Lucy, and she started to squirm a little in the awkwardness of it all. Then he looked back at Lucy's grandma. "I am going to town tomorrow to see a movie. Tucker got his license and we are driving to the movie theatre at the park." Lucy looked stunned as the conversation continued.

"Wait," she interrupted, "There is a movie theatre here?!"

"Not exactly," Grandma replied. "The church brings their projector outside weekly for a movie in the park. They put a big white sheet up over there by the promenade. It's a lovely event. I don't go often, but maybe Tucker could come pick you up."

"Tucker is my twin brother," Ethan said. "Well, we aren't identical or anything. Yes, we can do that – I will answer for him. Be ready at 4pm on Saturday." He grabbed the box and began to walk away, then turned around. "Please make sure you are ready, because we won't wait – I don't want to miss the movie – it's an illegal showing of Star Wars. You know, Disney does not condone what we do, but we do it anyway. We just hope they won't sue the church if they find out."

With that he toddled off. Grandma laughed and ordered the pizza. Lucy had grown to appreciate Casey's pizza. It had the monopoly on *fastish* food. After they ate, Grandma asked if Lucy would drive her home. Lucy, glad to have some semblance of normal, jumped in and drove them home, chattering on about what she had read and her time at the park. Grandmas smiled as if she had some secret plan playing out in her head and Lucy was just a piece of the story.

After they got home Grandma, went in and fell asleep in her chair. An outing and the air had made her tired. Lucy hurried out to the porch swing and pulled out the journal.

Today is the big day - I am leaving for college. Christopher and Laura asked if David could drive me to Springfield since their car probably would not carry us all. I am glad to have some time with him. He has become such a dear friend, and

A Ride Down the Road ©2019

it will be good to talk. I am concerned that our friendship is growing too much... I can't have that, not with James waiting for me in Springfield. I want so badly to be in that town with people and lights. I do love the countryside, the peacefulness and the people, but a bit of me misses the excitement – the atmosphere of a city.

January was an awful time to be going to Springfield, but the semester classes started in a few days and she needed to move into her dorm.   There was not much snow this year on the ground. It just looked brown with puddles of white and the naked branches of the trees waving slowly with the wind. David's gloved hands gripped the steering wheel as they drove down the road.

"Are you excited about college?" he asked, glancing over at his bundled companion. The truck got them where they needed to go, but it was never really warm inside.

"I am! I am eager to learn and gain a certificate. What an opportunity for a girl like me to be able to do this, right?" she said, looking out the window

"A girl like you?" he asked, turning to her with a puzzled look.

"Well, you know, an orphan who really has nothing of her own. I am cared for by the generosity of my cousin and this town. I am forever in their debt." Grace replied.

"Grace, you know that they don't feel that way. Laura and Christopher love you and would do anything for you. Never think of yourself as 'a girl like you'. You are smart and talented and the town sees that and that's why they entrusted you with this opportunity. University is an amazing thing, it was one of the best times of my life."

Grace always enjoyed her time with David. He had a way of phrasing things that made her *think,* yet never making her feel as though he was talking down to her. He treated her as an equal, which felt odd, and it was something she had never experienced before. She pulled the sleeve of her red coat down past her wrists. Her gloves were black leather, a gift from a student this year for her journey.

"You went to college? I never knew you went to college, what did you study?"

"Mathematics, and I enjoyed it very much. I even considered becoming a professor or following in my father's footsteps and running a business, but I didn't want that for my family." David said.

"You didn't want money and comfort?" Grace teased.

"No," he chuckled, "It's not that – I mean, money is fine, but to get that money a lot of people sacrifice a lot of things. They travel and work long hours sitting at a desk. My father spent more time working than anyone I know… he traveled and kept to himself a lot. Plus, he drank to relax because he couldn't seem to relax otherwise. Most of the time, he was fine, but sometimes, he drank too much," David revealed, his voice trailing off as he gripped the steering wheel a bit tighter. Grace reached over and touched his forearm. The muscle tensed then relaxed beneath her hand. She wasn't sure what to say or whether to ask him more. By his expression, he looked frustrated, but his voice was cool and steady as he cleared his throat and continued.

"It just wasn't for me. He wasn't a bad person, he was brilliant and did a lot of good for a lot of people. The business afforded us a lot of luxuries that many could not dream of… I am not bitter about it and loved him very much. I looked up to him and all he achieved. I just didn't want that… I like to be outside and to be with my boys… just a different dream." David confided.

David's ability to remain calm and steady always impressed Grace. She appreciated that about him when there were tense situations at church meetings (or anything, really). He seemed to always remain calm and focused.

"David are you happy?" she asked, glancing across the bench seat at her friend.

"Happy?" he asked, shooting her a grin, "Yes, I have to say 'yes'. I am taking my friend to college and…" She lightly smacked his forearm and rolled her eyes

"Well, it *is* a joyous occasion," he chuckled.

"Well, I am quite happy about it," she said, wiping her skirt with her hands as if to sweep out the wrinkles. "James seems less happy with it." She glanced over to see if David's expression changed at the mention of James' name. She knew that David told Christopher and Laura that he did not think that James was a good match for Grace. He told them that there was more there that he didn't trust.

At one of James' few visits to the house was during a Sunday lunch the men had a tense conversation.

James and David had a disagreement over lunch about farms and business. James believed that farmers needed to increase their land ownership using loans and support from a bank. He asserted that even though farmers were not great business people, they could be assisted with the right bank partnership, and that if they did not pay, the bank increased their asset. David believed that living within your means may mean having a smaller farm for a time, but the profits could grow slowly. A person leveraging themselves too far leads to difficult situations and then he quoted scripture as backing about wise and foolish people.

"James believes that it's a nice *idea* for me to attend college, but that it's not necessary for me to continue teaching… later." Grace stated.

Concern drifted across David's face as he asked, "But what do *you* want? Do you love teaching? And the kids? I mean, going to university is a valuable thing, regardless of how you use the education – you should pursue what you love."

"Like you?" she laughed.

"Yes, I gained a lot from my degree – math is an easily-applied skill. Plus, I met Albert's & Ben's mother, and I don't know where I would be without them. All good things… all good things."

"But their mother wasn't good – she *left* you!" shot back Grace, without thinking.

As soon as she spoke, she wished she could grab the words in mid-air and pull them back into her mouth. There was a long silence in the cab as she froze, waiting for David's response. She twisted the sleeve of her blue cardigan from under the sleeve of her coat, then looked out the window at the barren landscape. The ground was brown and dead.

"I'm sorry," she said, breaking the silence. She looked over and touched his arm again. She truly did not mean to hurt her friend.

David gazed straight ahead as he calmly replied, "Grace, everyone knows she left me. She wanted more than to be a farmer's wife and to raise children. She wanted something I could not give her. She made it clear that I would never be enough…" He rubbed the steering wheel, his voice breaking a bit with emotion, "That the boys would never be enough… and it was true: No one would ever *make* her happy."

She watched him as he spoke. The lines at the edges of his eyes never left, but when he smiled, his eyes smiled, too. He glanced over and looked at her. "Happiness, as I have learned, is a choice. It's just an emotion, nothing more. In spite of circumstances, we can have joy. Joy is just contentment wrapped in a smile. Joy is knowing that, despite our lack, that God's plan is always good."

The cab was again silent as Grace absorbed the words. Then he continued, "Remember that someday, you will need it. Christopher was speaking truth when he preached about how the rains come often, not once...building your house on the rock is building your foundation on something solid - something that lasts a lifetime."

They spent the remainder of the trip chatting about anything and everything – just like always, without a lull or pause.

They pulled into the college campus, beautiful with its tall trees and stone edged walkways. The buildings were made of stone and had thick, rounded, double wooden doors clad with black metal handles. They drove until they found the women's dormitory, and David parked the truck. They both sat in the truck and stared at the building.

"So, this is home," Grace said, taking a deep breath and clutching her small handbag.

"No," David replied gently, putting his hand on her shoulder. "This is where you will stay for a while during school. *Home* is where your family is...and we will be at the parsonage." Then he got out to retrieve her suitcase from the back of the truck.

As he did, she looked down and closed her eyes. So much change and so many blessings. How quickly life had changed for her -- now she had opportunities... and family. Never could she have imagined, sitting in church in New York after the fire, what life would be, that *this* was what was waiting for her around the bend . She had been sitting there, sobbing, wrapped in a soft quilt given to her by a church member. The sweet woman just held her as she cried, as if to absorb every ounce of pain that her tears let out.   The woman had been a light in the storm, stroking her hair softly and singing, "His eye is on the sparrow… and I know He watches me." The flashback sent tears tumbling down her cold cheeks. As David opened the door, she quickly wiped the tears away.

"Are you ok?" he asked.

"Yes," she replied. "Just taking a big breath before I step into the unknown."

A Ride Down the Road ©2019

"Would you like me to carry this in for you? Make sure you get settled and find your way?" he asked, as she stepped out of the truck. College students bustled past them, in and out of buildings. They were all wrapped in jackets and scarves, even though the day was unseasonably warm for January.

"No," she said, smiling and taking the suitcase from him. "I can do it."

They stood there for a long moment, staring at one another, until David broke the silence. He cleared his throat and said, "If you ever need anything at all, remember that you can call Garret's store and that they will get ahold of me or Christopher, you know how to do that, right? We would be here very quickly."

"Thank you – yes, I remember. Laura grilled me before I left." Grace replied, as she smiled at her friend.

David looked down. "Well… goodbye, then." He said, as he turned and walked away to get in the truck.

"David!" she said, setting down her suitcase. She ran to him and threw her arms around his neck, hugging him close. Her head rested on his shoulder as they stood in the cool wind. She could feel his warm breath as he hugged her tightly and whispered in her ear. "I meant that… I will be here in a heartbeat if you need me."

"I know…" she replied, not wanting the hug to end. When she finally let go, she reached up and touched his cheek. For a moment, she thought he might lean in and kiss her and she would have welcomed it. Is it possible to fall for someone while you are in love with someone else?

Reaching up and taking her hand from his face, he smiled. He gave her one last long look, then wearily turned and left.

A Ride Down the Road ©2019

~ Chapter 9 ~

Saturday afternoon! Lucy could hardly contain herself. She and Grandma filled a green Tupperware full of cookies to share at the movie in the park. They laughed as they laid parchment paper between each layer of cookies and filled it to where the curled lid could hardly close. Usually, the container sat with one of several in the freezer, full of cookies. Lucy always knew where to go to find a delectable bite. She couldn't decide whether the rock-hard, frozen cookies or the fresh-out-of-the-oven cookies were her favorite, so she just happily indulged in both.

The clock sang "cuckoo" from the other room as the bird jumped out and the people danced in a circle. Lucy hurried back to her room and threw on her favorite Royals hat, pulling her ponytail through the back. She heard the doorbell and ran to the family room, slowing as a voice greeted her Grandma.

"Grandma!" said an unfamiliar voice as she walked in the room. She was shocked, expecting to see the blond-haired boy from Casey's, but was instead greeted by the tall, handsome guy from the green truck. His Cardinals hat was in his hand, revealing a mop of wavy brown hair and a giant smile.

"Hi!" he said, stepping towards her and extending his hand for a shake. "I'm Tucker."

"You don't look like your twin," she stuttered, taking his hand and shaking it.

Tucker looked confused, then laughed as he replied, "Ethan? Well, we aren't exactly twins… more like, well" He chuckled and looked up at the ceiling. "Well… we are step-brothers no genetics, but Ethan has been claiming me as his twin since we were five."

A Ride Down the Road ©2019

"Oh!" Lucy exclaimed, as the two awkwardly laughed. Grandma looked at the two of them and smiled. They were stuck in a strange zone of tongue-tied silence.

"Well, you two should probably get going. The movie won't wait!" Grandma said, as she ushered her stunned granddaughter towards the door. Tucker stepped aside and let her go first, then leaned down and let Grandma kiss his forehead.

"Oh! Wait!" Lucy said as she hurried back to the kitchen to get the tub of cookies. She tossed it to an enthusiastic Tucker. "Oh yeah!" Tucker said, tucking them under his arm like a Heisman trophy statue. "I will have to keep these for myself!" he joked, hustling out the door to the truck.

Lucy stood by the side of the truck, admiring its smooth lines. It had wooden guards lining the edge of the bed. It looked like something out of a museum, not the truck of a 17-year-old boy. She smiled as she ran her hand along the side of it.

"It's great, huh?" Tucker asked, as he jogged down the walkway and quickly opened her door. She climbed inside as he handed her the cookie container and continued, "She was a *mess* when I got her."

He slammed her door shut, then ran around to climb in the driver's seat.

"I am sorry, I didn't know it was unlocked," Lucy said, after he buckled his seat belt and put the car in reverse. He carefully checked behind him before backing out of the driveway.

"No one locks their cars here," he said with a grin, keeping his eyes on the road as he turned the wheel to align the truck with the dirt road leading out to civilization. "Who would steal *this* baby, anyway?!" he laughed, "everyone knows who she belongs to." He rubbed his hand along the dash, then put the truck into drive, slowly pulling down the street. He waved as he honked the horn. Lucy hadn't even realized that Grandma was standing on the front porch, wrapped in her evening shawl. Lucy waved and smiled, hoping that Grandma would not be waiting up for her tonight.

"So you restored it?" Lucy asked, looking over at her very focused driver.

"Yes, it was covered with a tarp and it would've just rusted out and died under there if I hadn't taken it off her hands. I spent a whole year restoring it with my stepdad," Tucker boasted, beaming with pride. "It's a 'resto-mod', which means that we used as much of the original car as we could, then added new things like power steering and a new engine."

"It's great! I like it a lot. My grandma gave me a box of old letters and journals, and there is an old truck in some of them. It's like stepping back in time though this whole town seems that way," Lucy shared.

"Oh! I *live* back in time! My mom is a junk gypsy. She loves to buy old stuff, and I am her moving company. I think that was why she gave me the money to get the truck finished up. She needed someone to haul her stuff," Tucker said.

"I liked the shop. I went inside and read for a while. The window display is very cool. I liked the plates. Is your whole house like that?"

"Kind of, my mom and dad don't always agree on decorations. Though my mom wins often, my dad sometimes puts his foot down. So the shop is her outlet," he said, raising one hand up in the air and waving it like a queen. "A woman needs her creative space."

"I thought you said you have a stepdad?" Lucy asked, laughing at his impersonation.

"I do and I call him 'Dad'. My bio-dad isn't around very much. He is not a bad guy or anything, just makes some…

uh… *interesting* choices…and, you know, he isn't around too much. My stepdad, well, he is really a great guy. And he is good to my mom."

Lucy wanted to grill him on what it was like to have divorced parents and how he dealt with the split, but she didn't really know him well enough. Instead, she smoothly changed the subject to something more entertaining.

"So, who got you that awful red hat?" Lucy asked, motioning towards his cap.

"What? This hat?" he said, pointing to his head and laughing. "You are making fun of my team? You have never even seen us play!"

"You play for the Cardinals?" she laughed, wanting to grab the hat from his head and toss it out the window where it belonged, but didn't for fear of disrupting his driving.

"Yes, as a matter of fact, I do. I play first base and sometimes pitch when they need a closer."   He grinned, knowing that he was making her crazy.

"Is it your club team or something?" she asked.

"No, it's the high school team. We are the Cardinals." Tucker chanted.

"Well…" she started, giggling as she spoke, "I could never go to school here. That would be like a daily betrayal to the boys in blue, and I just couldn't bring myself to be that type of person."

"Betrayal! Die hard, are you? Truth be known, I *do* like the Royals. In fact, next year will be my last year in red… I graduate and hope to get a scholarship to play somewhere so I can go to college." Tucker said, taking off his hat and sitting it on the seat.

"What will you study?" Lucy asked, watching the countryside fly by outside the window.

"Business, I guess, it applies to lots of things, so I can work anywhere if I want to later," He replied, "What about you?"

"I don't know yet. Maybe music or writing or something… probably less practical and less useful. That will make my parents nuts, but it would make me happy," Lucy said picking up his hat and examining it.

The two conversed and laughed all the way to the park. The park was filled with people on their blankets, some with picnic baskets. Children ran in and out of the blankets like it was an obstacle course. Laughter and conversations rose like smoke from a campfire. Tucker parked the truck and guided Lucy towards the free hot dogs and cotton candy. Eventually, they found Ethan and took a seat with him on the blanket.

The Pastor stood and talked to the crowd before the movie started, thanking the church members who helped set things up. He talked a lot about how a church is a family and how they really showed up that way. He ended by saying, "There's a lot of truth in Star Wars Movies. Not truth like' Ewoks are real' but Biblical themes of sacrificing for others and the battle of good vs evil. But what I see is more than that... it's about people who make choices that influence the course of their lives. Good or bad, each step is a choice down a path. It also tells me that you can never be too far gone to make a choice towards turning to good. The gospel is like that… the door is always open to anyone who is looking to choose a better path, but it's a choice, and only you can make it."

As the movie played, Lucy relaxed on the blanket and started to daydream about what she had read earlier in Grace's letters.

Dear Laura,

My classes are so difficult, but I have been enjoying the challenge. I appreciate the new scarf. It is beautiful and I have worn it every day. The wind is so bitter cold here. Thank you for the money, as well. Please thank the congregation for me. I have made a few friends, but it is difficult. Conversations seem to go to family, and when they ask me, there are lots of questions... it's just easier to stay quiet. It breaks my heart to speak of my mother... and it makes me homesick to speak of you. I miss our talks and our walks. I miss the school and the kids. I even miss the sermons.

I want so badly to be accepted in these circles, for them not to see me as an orphan or as some charity case. I know God has a plan for me and I know it is good. I do appreciate all that you have done for me and all that the town has done. I just want to be normal like the others here.

James is a dream. He is handsome and successful and he is intelligent. He tells me often how he thinks I am beautiful and special to him. No one has ever talked to me the way he does, and I look forward to every word.

James has been very good to come and pick me up from school on occasion for dinner or for an outing. We have been to several lovely places. Yesterday, he sent his driver to pick me up because he was running late at work, and I went to his home, where his cook had prepared a meal.

Grace followed the driver into the craftsman-style house that was hidden behind a church. The chandelier sparkled, its crystals reflecting small rainbows on the ceiling. The stairs hugged the wall and were clad with leaded-glass windows.

"Can I take your coat, Miss?" the driver asked. He was a tall black man with a long, thin face and kind smile.

"Yes, thank you," Grace said, taking off her coat and handing it to him. He disappeared into a small coat closet to hang things up. Grace could hear the sounds of dishes clanking and someone singing softly. She walked slowly towards the sounds and delicious smells and found herself in the kitchen. An older black woman was sitting at the table peeling potatoes and singing.

"Hello," Grace said, startling the woman, who nearly knocked the bowl of potatoes off the table.

"You must be Miss Grace," The woman said, jumping to her feet. She smiled as she walked towards her. "Now you go on and get outta here, go wait in the parlor for Mr. James. He will be home soon."

Grace looked through the door at the empty parlor, then sat down at the table in the kitchen. "I have been quiet all day long. I could be helpful. I have peeled potatoes before."

"Ohhh, Mr. James would not like that. You should go sit in the parlor," the woman said trying to encourage her to leave.

"Please, I want to be helpful. I would like to get to know you. Please," Grace pleaded.   The woman reluctantly sat down and handed her a knife and a potato.

"Don't skin them too thick, we don't waste here," she said, as she looked at Grace whittling away at the potato.

"What is your name?" Grace asked, her eyes focused on her work.

"Luella," she replied, shaking her head a bit at Grace's peeling job and eyeing the uneven skin.

"How long have you worked here?" Grace continued, focusing her efforts, and trying to imitate Luella's long, spirally peels of skin.

"I have worked for Mr. James' family my whole life. My mama worked for him before me. They have been good to us through the years." LuElla added.

A Ride Down the Road ©2019

"Is your mama here?" Grace asked.

"No Miss, my mama is with the Lord. She died a few years ago," LuElla confided. Grace stopped peeling and looked at her companion.

"I am sorry to hear that, my mother died, too. I miss her," Grace lamented. "Sometimes I wonder how long it will hurt."

"You will always miss her, the pain never really leaves. Some days, I still wake up and forget that she has gone home to be with Jesus… I just want to talk to her. You know, the way a child talks to her mama is special," LuElla shared, "but remember you will see her again. It's never Good-Bye, it's just I will see you later."

They continued their conversation about their mothers and memories. Joy filled the kitchen, and Grace felt connected to her in a way that she had not felt with many people.

The door opened abruptly, and James appeared. He took off his hat and set it on the table's edge.

"Grace, what are you doing in here?" he asked, frowning at LuElla.

"Mr. James, I told her to go sit in the parlor and that gurl don't listen," she said, smiling at Grace and taking the knife away.

"I didn't want to sit by myself," Grace replied as she stood up and wiped her hands on the embroidered feed sack towel that LuElla had given her.

"You two go on now, and I will get supper finished up and on the table." LuElla said waving them into the other room.

James escorted Grace through the butler's pantry and into the parlor, then spun her around and kissed her. She welcomed his embrace and closeness. She felt less alone the more she spent time with him. She held his hand and followed as he walked towards the cherrywood bar. He took a tumbler and poured a glass of scotch.

"How were your classes today?" he asked, taking a sip of scotch.

"They were difficult, but no matter. I finished my homework so I could focus on you this evening. What kept you so long?" she asked, as she stepped away from him to look at the painting on the wall. His parlor was nicely appointed with high ceilings, crown molding, and decorative paintings. A cozy fire crackled in the fireplace.

The painting that Grace gazed at was of a path in the woods on a fall day. The light trickled in through the branches, illuminating the clearing. She wondered where the path went. On the right and left, there were dark, wooded areas. On the path branches and ruts were visible because of the light showing the way. It reminded her of a teaching Laura gave one day on a scripture: "No matter where you go, to the right or to the left, your ears will hear… *this* is the way. Walk in it," she said using hand motions to act out her words.

James flipped on the radio, then poured himself a glass as the music played. He walked over to Grace and slipped his hand around her small waist, resting it in the curve.

"Do you like this one?" he asked, sipping his drink.

"Yes," she replied, keeping her eyes fixed on the painting. "The colors remind me of home. The hills were the most beautiful thing I have ever seen. The woods are so vast, and there are clearings like this, where the trees make caves."

"The artist is a friend of my mother. Her family and mine are… close. She sometimes comes to town. Maybe, next time, I can introduce you," he murmured.

"It would be nice to meet your parents sometime, too." Grace said, as she turned from the painting and faced him. Usually, this request made James squirm, but this time, he smiled. He sat his drink down on the table, then wrapped his arms around his catch.

"Well, I have a proposition for you." James said pulling her closer, "really, an invitation from the governor himself! They are having a dinner in March – it's really a nice affair with several very important and influential people. I would like to bring you as my guest."

Grace smiled from ear to ear. His dark eyes twinkled as he continued on, "it will be at the governor's mansion. It's a very formal event."

Grace had determined that this was a next, very important, step in their relationship. He had met her family several times in his visits. Christopher and Laura did not seem thrilled with him. They felt his faith was questionable and his intentions were not always in the right place. Laura had many conversations with her about it, cautiously asking Grace, "Does he help you love God more? Does he help you seek Jesus?" Grace always replied with a "yes" and told her cousin he challenged her faith so much it made her seek to learn more. She knew that it wasn't a good encouragement towards God. She rationalized that even a contentious encouragement was still encouragement. Laura's discernment always amazed Grace.

She had received a recent letter from her that read, *"Whoever you chose should help you love God more and lead you, the way a gentle shepherd would. Marriage can be difficult. Aligning two different people with habits and ideals is not easy. Your future husband needs to be focused on Jesus so that he can love you the way Jesus loved the church – willing to lay down his life for her."*

"It is important to me that they..." James started but was interrupted.

A Ride Down the Road ©2019

"Mr. James," LuElla's voice called from the kitchen, "Supper is on the table."

"Thank you, LuElla," he said, stepping back with a bow to allow Grace to walk in front of him to the dining room.

Grace had never eaten at James' home before. The dining room, though not incredibly large or stately, was beautiful. It had mahogany wood casing on the walls and the rest painted a lovely French blue. There were more paintings in this room that hung from the picture rail at the ceiling. The table was set with beautiful blue and white china, and their plates were placed at opposite ends of the dining table. Candles burned, and the lights overhead were low. James walked with Grace and pulled out her chair. She loved how he did things like that. He stood when she got up from the table, opened doors, and always pulled out chairs for her to sit down. He offered his arm when they left a location and ordered her dinner at restaurants.

"James, what would I need to wear to an event like this? I am concerned," she started.

"I don't want you to worry. We will go to town and buy you whatever dress you would like and all the accessories," he said, smiling as he sat down across from her. Grace was delighted with the idea of a new frock. She had not had something new in a long time. While she was thankful for the generosity of others to cover her basic needs, it would be so nice to have something special. James was always bringing her flowers, candies, and, even once, a locket that she wore always.

"Grace, whatever you want! I will always provide it for you. That's my job," James said, taking a bite of his meal. Grace was overwhelmed with joy as she thought about the dress. As dinner progressed, they chatted about the color and style. Grace giggled and delighted in his ideas and thoughts. He told her about all of the people who would attend and their attention to detail. She was nervous in some ways, worried that she wouldn't meet the approval of his family and friends.

A Ride Down the Road ©2019

But James dismissed her concerns by assuring her that he would get her a fine dress, and that there was nothing at all to worry about.

However, Grace knew that gaining the approval of *some* took more than just a nice dress. She had seen people in New York and on the train with judgmental eyes. She wasn't sure that she could impress the crowd he was describing, no matter what she wore.

~ Chapter 10 ~

Lucy spent the morning filling her Grandma in on details of the outing to the movies.

"Like – I know it was not a date or anything but he is so handsome, and he is a pitcher! I mean, really, Grandma, you couldn't find a way to tell me that there are handsome guys out here in the middle of nowhere?!" Lucy jabbered.

Grandma smiled as she ate her biscuits and gravy. It was Lucy's favorite meal; she could eat it at any time of day. Restaurant biscuits and gravy had *nothing* on Grandma. Real grease, real sausage, real homemade from scratch biscuits! What more could a girl ask for?

"You need to eat, child your food is getting cold," Grandma said. Her silver hair caught the sun from the back door and seemed to sparkle. Lucy smiled. She loved being here and loved her Grandma. It was different this time than the last – maybe she was older, or maybe it was because she was on her own.

The phone broke the happy silence and stopped Lucy from shoveling the food in her mouth for a moment. She leaned her chair back on two legs and grabbed the phone.

"Hello!" she sang into the phone. "Mom! Oh, hi, Mom! I have to tell you about my evening – I …. Yes, she is here ...yes, we are finishing breakfast, but I want to tell you about the movie and riding in this old truck...yes ...yes…I guess I understand..." All Lucy remembered next was her mom saying how much both she and her father loved her. Words kept coming through the phone's speaker into her ear, but none of them made sense. It was as if her mom was talking in another language, with Lucy only understanding bits and pieces. Separate homes...tired of trying… divorce. Lucy thought that they were going away for a marriage counseling thing, but they had gone away to figure out the divorce. They "couldn't make it work" and "hated it was this year", but they were both done with being married.

A Ride Down the Road ©2019

How does that happen, anyway? How do people who say they love each other suddenly be "done"? Lucy stood in the kitchen with the phone to her ear, staring at the milk glass cake plate full of cookies. It had a ruffled edge and small raised dots. She reached and took one -- then another -- as her mom continued. She rambled on -- something about picking her up soon and letting set up her new room. Her grandma sat at the table watching her, unable to help as her world crumbled.   Grandma got up went to the fridge, grabbed a bottle of milk, and filled up an empty jelly jar glass. She pushed the white cake plate full of cookies towards her. Lucy rocked back in the handmade chair and ran her hand along the smooth edge of the round maple table. It matched the hutch in the corner where Grandma stored her special dishes.

Over and over, her mom rattled on, talking about happiness and how she just wasn't happy anymore. Lucy found herself staring at the dishes in the hutch, studying them as her mom kept talking. They had a pale-yellow rim and small multicolored flowers in clusters around the edges. The pink and blue flowers flanked the larger yellow ones and were accented with tiny purple dainty flowers floating around the bouquet. The cups had the same design inside, revealing itself only as you finished your drink. "Yes... yes... I am listening..." Lucy said, returning to reality with a jolt. "Mom, can I stay here for a few more days... maybe even the rest of the month? There's no rush, right? I mean if it's ok with Grandma."

Grandma nodded quickly and smiled, whispering, "Of course, dear."

"Ok... that sounds good... Okay, Mom. I love you, too." With that, she hung up the phone and stared at her Grandma. It was as if her entire world had been rolling forward and slammed into wall. She didn't know how to speak.

"Lucy," Grandma said, breaking the silence.

"Did you know?" Lucy interrupted. The question hung in the air as they sat in silence for a moment, her grandma looking down at the table.

"I knew that they didn't think it would work. I knew they had a 'counselor', but maybe by that they meant 'lawyer'." Grandma replied, nervously gripping her glass of milk.

"They just lied to me! It's like when you tell a dog you are going for a ride, then take them to the vet to be put down. That's what they did!" Lucy said, shoving bite after bite of cookie in her mouth as tears started to well up in her eyes. Grandma jumped to her feet and wrapped her arms around her. "Why don't they love each other? Why can't they just stay married... for *me*?!"

"I don't know, dear. I just don't know. I am so sorry. I know this is hard and not what you want." Lucy's slow cry turned into a sob -- she cried so hard that her body shook. She had not cried this way for her parents yet. Her body seemed to expel tears at an uncontrollable rate. The tears splashed on the linoleum floor one by one.

"Grandma, I just want to live with you and not deal with their mess. It's my senior year… there's a school here. I could just move here and stay here." Lucy pleaded through her tears.

"Dear, I would love to have you, but I am not sure how that would go over with your folks." Grandma consoled.

"Forget them!" Lucy said, as she quickly wiped her eyes. "They only want what is best for *them*… they don't care about me! It's my senior year! I can probably emancipate myself and live anywhere I want!"

"Lucy, take a breath, dear. Let's let today's troubles be enough for today." Grandma pleaded.

"Stop quoting scripture to me, Grandma! Today's troubles are *way* more than just for today! It's my whole life." Lucy

A Ride Down the Road ©2019

replied angrily. "Happiness... that's all they want? What about *me*?! I have no control over any of this!"   Lucy shared with disdain.

"Lucy," her grandma started, then seemed to be at a loss of words as she looked at her granddaughter.

"I am going for a walk in the field," Lucy said, grabbing her satchel and letting the screen door slam behind her. She ran through the backyard and climbed over the metal fence. She followed the truck ruts in the ground to the top of the hill and surveyed the field. The cows were by the pond, their feet sinking in at the edges as they leaned in for a morning drink.   In the middle of the field was a grove of trees. Lucy decided that would be her spot for today. It would be a good spot to think.   As she walked through the field, she thought of Grace and how she walked through fields like this as she tried to figure out what to do with her life. Grace's problems didn't seem as daunting as Lucy's right now.

Lucy found her spot next to a tree and sat down, opening the journal to the latest page.

James took me shopping today downtown. The ladies fawned over me in the store and I felt like a model. Each dress seemed more elegant than before. The fringe and ruffles – the beading and crystals... it was like nothing I have ever experienced before in my life. He came with me and was my cheering section for the event. I have never had anything so nice before in my life. It's not that I don't appreciate all of the kindness of the town donating clothing to me. I really do! It's just nice to have something so beautiful.   He purchased the dress, matching shoes, and a hat! Then we walked to a restaurant for dinner.

Downtown, it seemed as though everyone had cars. Everything seemed to move so quickly, and Grace was a bit overwhelmed. Maybe country life had infected her and cured her of the need for the hustle and bustle she had grown up with in New York.

As James walked into the restaurant he we greeted by the man at the front, "Ah! Mr. Carter – what a pleasure to see you! Would you like your table by the window?"

"Yes, George, thank you," James replied, removing his coat and handing it to the other gentleman.

"This is Grace, and she will be joining me tonight." James said, as he put his hand on the small of her back and ushered her forward.

"Any friend of yours is a friend of ours!" The man replied as he motioned to his helper to take her coat.

"Thank you," she said, making sure to make eye contact with the young man, who then nodded in acknowledgement and returned her smile.

Grace had observed James several times at fine restaurants. He never seemed to acknowledge the servers. He explained that it is their job to be invisible and that she was insulting them by speaking to them. Grace could never bring herself to not show appreciation, so she did it as discreetly as possible.

They walked across the restaurant, the other patrons turning to take note of them. Grace was used to people stopping to speak to James because of his position. Dinner was frequently interrupted by people stopping by to say hello and exchanging niceties. However, she also noticed how women seemed to be drawn to him. His charming smile often captured their attention. Women would just come up and start talking to him as if Grace was not even with him. When she mentioned this to him, he'd dismiss her fears, often by reminding her that she didn't need to worry about it, because he was *leaving* with *her*.

James had three drinks during their meal. The server filled his glass as if it were water instead of brandy. They talked about the dress and the day.

A Ride Down the Road ©2019

"You would look amazing in a potato sack," James said, as he motioned the waiter, tapping the side of his glass for a refill.

"You are too kind to me," Grace replied, then timidly added, "James… don't you think you've had enough to drink?" She laughed nervously, "I'm not a very good driver, and you still have to get yourself home."

James smiled slyly as he slightly stuttered his response, "If it bothers you, then I will stop." He waved away the server and continued, "Are you ready to go?"

He signed the bill and left a generous tip. As they walked to the door, the host quickly had the coats retrieved, and James tipped both workers. Grace enjoyed watching his generosity, and she jumped in to join him by expressing her gratitude numerous times. They hurried back to his car, and he opened the door for her. As the ignition fired up, they laughed at their frozen breath that hung like smoke in the brisk February air.

"Would you like to come to my house to watch the new television?" he asked, smiling at her and touching her frozen nose.

"A television? You have a television?!" she exclaimed. "Yes, yes, I'd love to see it!" Even though it was late, she could not resist the opportunity to see the fascinating new addition to his parlor.

"I thought you might," he laughed, as he pulled away from the restaurant. He swerved a bit on the road, but then steadied the car. "I got it … I got it." He smiled as he reached over and took her hand with one of his, bringing it to his mouth and kissing it lightly.

She chattered all the way to his house. He seemed in good spirits, and, despite the many drinks, was able to make it home with little issue. Inside, they rushed into the parlor where he revealed the large wooden box that housed a

A Ride Down the Road ©2019

small rounded screen. Grace ran her hand across the front of the box and knelt in front of it.

"Amazing," she said softly, as she smiled at James' reflection in the glass. She stood quickly and hugged him. "It's amazing! I am so excited! How does it work?"

James turned the television on, then put the channel on NBC. They watched in wonder as the "Railroad Hour" musicians, singers and dancers graced the stage. The music was so inviting that James pulled her close, and they danced across the parlor floor. James periodically leaned in for a quick kiss or two. He spun her one more time, then walked to the radio and poured two glasses of brandy.

"Here, would you like one?" he asked Grace, holding out a small glass.

"Oh no…" she laughed, "I can't do that. I don't drink, you know that."

"I insist, try it!" he said, handing her the glass. She smelled it, wrinkling her nose as it burned from the alcohols' fumes.

"Really, James, I don't want to," she insisted, handing it back to him. As he reached out to take it, the glass tipped, spilling the brandy down the front of her shirt.

"Oh no!" she cried out in alarm.

"Oh, I am sorry let me get you a towel," he said, as he grabbed a small napkin then attempted to dry her shirt with it, taking full advantage of the spill.

"James!" she giggled, snatching the napkin and turning her back to him. He finished off his drink and set it on the end table, then wrapped his arms around her from behind and swayed to the music.

"I am a mess," she said, swaying with him as she continued to wipe her shirt. He leaned down and started to kiss the back of her neck.

"Maybe we should wash your shirt," he said, running his hand down her side and tugging on the edge of her blouse. She dropped the napkin and grabbed his hands, trying to keep her shirt in place. "No no…" she giggled. "No, that won't be necessary. I can clean it when I get to the dorm."

He pulled her close and started to kiss her more passionately than normal. He sat her on the coach and began to run his hand down the side of her skirt to the base, lifting it slowly as his hand touched her leg.

"James…" she said between kisses, "James, stop…" Her hands raced to stop his invasion. She was so overwhelmed, fear mixed with passion swept over her. She knew she had to stop and that it wasn't right to give in, but she was struggling.

"I love you…" He said between kisses. "Grace… I love you and want to spend the rest of my life with you."

He continued to pursue her, and the intensity in the room grew. She could hardly will herself to say it again. "Stop… please… James..." Suddenly, fear swept over her. She was not ready for this, and it was outside of her commitment to herself. She needed it to stop. "James! Stop!" she cried, as forcefully as she could, pushing him with all of her strength. The full weight of his body was holding her down. "James! Please! I don't want to do this!"

He continued, despite her pleas. Tears began to run down her flushed cheeks. "James, I don't want to do this. Please stop… please…" Tears turned into full-blown sobs, and she struggled to free herself from him.

Suddenly, the phone rang, and the familiar voice of LuElla called from the kitchen. "Mr. James. Sir, it's your father, Mr. James!"

James stopped and exhaled slowly. "I will be right there, LuElla." As he pulled away from Grace, he noticed she was crying.

"Why are you crying?" he asked, seeming surprised and a bit annoyed.

Grace quickly wiped her eyes as she replied, "I am ok... I just wanted you to stop and you didn't, and it scared me."

"Grace," he said annoyed, "I love you... wait here. I need to go and answer the call."

Grace sat quietly on the couch in the parlor and smoothed the wrinkles on her dress, then walked to the mirror to inspect her reflection. She dried off her face, refastened her hair tie, and tried to mask any sign of disarray. She noticed that the stain of the alcohol seemed to have grown larger across her chest.

"What are you doing?" she asked her reflection. Without prompting, it seemed to answer her back, "Not the right thing! You need to get yourself together! What are you doing at a man's house alone?! "

Soon, James returned, walking briskly across the room to close the brandy cabinet.

"We need to get you back. I must go into the bank," he explained, smoothing his hair and straightening his tie.

"It's so late..." Grace replied, nervously wringing her hands. He watched her for a moment, then smiled.

"Never play poker with anyone, my love, you have a tell when you are nervous," he said, walking towards her and taking her hands in his. "I love you, and this is just what people in love do. I didn't mean to make you uncomfortable. I just can't keep my mind off of you. I find it difficult to wait... you are irresistible to me."

A Ride Down the Road ©2019

Grace blushed and looked away, then smiled as he lightly grabbed her chin and redirected it to him. "I love you."

"I love you, too," she replied, as he leaned in and kissed her gently. Grace was so confused. Her emotions said there was nothing wrong with expressing her love to him physically, how he wanted her to, but her mind knew that it was not time.

"I'll take you home," he said, lightly touching her cheek.

~ Chapter 11 ~

Lucy sat under a tree; her thoughts consumed with the morning call. It made her think of the green book her mother used to read her, the one about the giving tree that just wanted the boy to be happy. Her parents' divorce was not a gift she wanted to be given.

"Can I give it back?" she asked out loud, as if she was talking to the tree or God or whomever happened to be listening. "I don't *want* this divorce."

She sat for hours, watching the sun make its way to the sky right above her head. It was hot, but the trees branches shaded her and kept her cool. It was a gift she welcomed.

Laying back on the ground she closed her eyes. Maybe if she fell asleep, she could wake up and this would all be a bad dream.

"Lucy… Lucy…" she heard a male voice call. It came from a distance, and at first, she thought she was actually dreaming. Then a dog barked. Suddenly, she heard trotting four-legged footsteps fast approaching, followed by a wet nose against her cheek. She opened her eyes to find a giant black lab hovering over her. Her handsome wavy-haired new friend was close behind.

"There you are! Grandma was worried, so she called me," Tucker said, as he sat down on the grass next to her.

Slowly, Lucy sat up. "I didn't mean to scare her. I just needed a little time to think," replied Lucy, still lying on her back and staring up at the sky. Tucker reached over and pulled a large leave from her hair.

"You want to talk about it?" he said, offering her the leaf with a sweet smile.

"Not really. I'm fine," Lucy replied, taking the leaf and studying its veins and edges before returning it to the ground. Hard to believe that so small would give something so large life.

"Listen, it's been a while ago, but I have been where you are, and if you need to talk we can. Let's face it. You are *not* 'fine' or 'okay' or 'good' or any other word you would use to describe yourself right now. It just sucks, and it's okay to say that – it's okay to *yell* it," Tucker said, wiping his hands on his baseball pants. He looked as if he had come from practice. She sat up and hugged her knees to her chest, then leaned her head to one side and ran her hands through the grass.

"Sometimes, it's just nice to hang out with someone who gets it – what it's like for your family to break apart, when you didn't ask for or want it," he continued, "Being in a divorced house is more than just the good stuff, you know: two birthdays and two Christmases," he smiled, nudging her softly. "You know, two cakes and two sets of presents isn't awful. But having to adjust to two families and two traditions… 'new traditions'… I hate that phrase. I liked our *old* traditions!"

Lucy shrugged and stared at the grass. Tucker glanced over to see the journal and letters spread out on the ground.

"You want to get out of here?" he asked. "Grandma made sandwiches, and they are in a cooler in my truck… if you want to, we could go and see the old parsonage… I can take you."

"Yes, I would love to go see it. Wait, how did you know about the parsonage? Have you read the journals?" Lucy inquired, intrigued by her new friend's revelation.

"No," he laughed, "But my mom did a while ago, and she talks about it all the time. Come on!" he grinned, standing to his feet and extending his hand to help her up. "Let's get outta here!"

She took his hand, letting him pull her to her feet. They grabbed her things and walked up the hill to the old truck. When Tucker opened the door for her, the strong smell of a boys' locker room came wafting out. He quickly grabbed his gym bag and threw it in the bed of the truck.

"Come on, Boomer!" He yelled, and the dog ran to him. Boomer happily climbed into the back of the truck barking at his owner. Lucy quickly rolled the window down, desperate for some fresh air, before she got into the truck.

"Sorry about that, I was at practice this morning when Grandma called, and I came straight here. You want lunch? It's in the cooler." Tucker said, motioning to the cooler.

Lucy opened the small blue lunch cooler to find three sandwiches, apples, and, of course, some cookies. She pulled out one and handed it to her driver, then took one for herself. They ate as they drove through the field and back to the farmhouse. Tucker quickly jumped out, sandwich in hand, and ran up to the front porch where Grandma sat. They spoke briefly, then she waved and blew kisses. He leaned down and she said something directly to his face, then sternly shook her finger and smiled.

"What did she say?" asked Lucy, as he got back into the truck.

"She said to be nice and to bring you home some time tonight," Tucker replied with a big grin. He took another bite of the sandwich and continued to the road.

"She is not very good at this teenager thing..." laughed Lucy, glancing over at him, amused by his oblivion to the mustard on his cheek.

They chatted off and on as they drove through the town and down Highway 13 towards the lake. Lucy loved the drive. The hills looked like fluffy green pillows on a giant oversized couch. Up and down, then around corners so tight that going faster than 20 miles an hour would have flung them over the

A Ride Down the Road ©2019

edge. Houses dotted the landscape. Some of them right on the edge of the cliff and others farther back.   Tucker turned down a deserted road, then stopped, hopped out, and opened up a gate.

"Where are we?" Lucy asked, as he got back in the car.

"Almost there!" he replied, shifting the truck into gear and pulling slowly down the narrow driveway. In a clearing was the house with 3 gables, now overgrown with vines. The porch had fallen down around the front door, hiding it from view. Some of the shutters hung delicately by one hinge and the others were clinging to the house, held only by the strength of the vine.

They got out of the truck and walked around the perimeter of the house, peering in windows as they talked. In the back, they stepped carefully around holes in the back porch, and Tucker forced open the unlocked door. Inside, the cupboards were still hanging on the wall, but some of the doors had come off. It was clear that new inhabitants had made their homes there. Lucy joked that it looked like a squirrel hotel. In the corner of the room, an old icebox was still nestled in a nook with rusty hinges and dirty wood.

They walked through the rounded doorway into the parlor. She imagined the people from the journal in the room… laughing… talking… sharing… being a family.

"It's like the journal has come to life," she said, running her hand along the wall.

"That's what my mom said when we found it," Tucker replied, moving an old chair over to the corner of the room.

"Are we going to get in trouble for trespassing?" Lucy asked, staring out the cracked window. It seemed a shame that the old bubbly glass would not be able to be repurposed or reused someday.

A Ride Down the Road ©2019

"Nah, I know the owner…" Tucker laughed, as he wiped some dust from the top of the mantle. "My mom bought it from Grandma. She is going to make it into a shop or bed and breakfast or something. It's supposed to be my project at some point to rebuild it, but, structurally, I am not sure how to do all of it."

They explored the inside of the house as much as they could. The entryway had a boxy stairwell with a dark, dirty wooden rail. Lucy started to take a step, but Tucker wouldn't let her go up because they were unsafe.

Outside the house, they found a trail that went to a clearing overlooking the Ozark hills and Table Rock Lake. The sunset was beautiful. The sky was a mixture of purples and pinks all the way to the blue water. They sat in silence as the sun started to set behind the hills.

"Did you bring the letters?" Tucker asked, looking over at Lucy.

"Yes," she said, smiling as she pulled the pile from the satchel.

"My mom read all of them to me…. she said there were a lot of good lessons to learn," he replied, sitting down on a fallen tree limb, then hopping back up in urgency. "I'd better get you back before Grandma starts to worry."

"I don't think she's worried knowing I'm with *you*," Lucy replied, as they walked carefully back down the path to the truck to head home. "Thanks for hanging out with me today," Lucy said, as they pulled into the driveway. They sat in silence for a bit.

"Lucy," Tucker said, "You need a friend right now… and I would like to be that friend. No strings attached, no expectations, just someone you can talk to."

"Thanks," she replied, as she got out of the truck and walked to the front porch. Tucker watched her let herself in, then

A Ride Down the Road ©2019

drove away. Alone in her room, Lucy pulled out the letters and picked up where she had left off.

Dear Laura,

I long to be home. I don't like the city – isn't that funny? I know it hasn't been too long since I left my own city life, but here it just feels overwhelming with all the hustle and bustle.
  The cars fill the streets here and there are lots of people hurrying to their next spot. No one seems to just stop and enjoy things. I have been ruined by the peacefulness of the mountains where we live. I miss sitting and watching the sunset and hearing nothing but birds and bugs. I even miss the bugs!

James is well, but he works many hours. When I first arrived, he seemed to have more time, but recently, his father has asked for support on a lot of things. He also said the bank is very busy working on a project with the Corps of Engineers. There are plans to let the lowlands flood for the creation of a recreational lake. I am concerned. My heart aches for some of the people in the area, but he insists that it's for the betterment of the region. How I hope he's right!

David wrote recently to tell me that Albert lost a tooth. He said that they are well and that the boys miss me. I miss them too.

I miss you especially our talks and your encouragement. I find myself challenged in so many ways with difficult choices. How did you make all the right choices? By the way, I am going to a dinner at the governor's home with James. I'll fill you in on all the details afterwards, of course. Wish you were here to help me with my hair!

Love you always,

Grace

Grace stood waiting with her bag in front of the college. She had been waiting for several minutes when James pulled up and jumped out of his car to greet her.

"Hello, my love!" he said, taking her suitcase, opening her door, and kissing her sweetly in one swift movement. "This will be an incredible weekend! You will love everything about it."

"I am really looking forward to meeting your parents!" Grace said, nervously stroking the satin hem of her new dress. The car began its forward motion. There was no turning back now. She was excited, but also anxious. James' parents were society people, and he had made mention several times of their high expectations for him. Their desires for success and position were very foreign to Grace. Her mother's only expectation in life was survival and finding as much happiness as could be found. "Grace, you know, my parents can be a little difficult, and I really need you to work hard to impress them," James said, as he leaned forward to check the traffic light.

"Difficult?" Grace asked, staring out the passenger window and pulling her shiny new purse close. She prayed that James wouldn't see her lips quiver.

"Well, you know, they are like any parent really. They want what is best for me and want me to be well-received in their circles. It's not always easy to gain approval. Their friends are the 'creme de la creme' of society. You know, successful, respected people." James said, in his way trying to reassure her.

Grace listened and watched James maneuver down the highway. The car grew quiet as she contemplated his words. Would they accept her or think she was worthy? And what about her lack of family and connections? She found herself praying that God would reveal the way for her to know that this was right. Soon, she felt a hand on hers and looked over at her smiling driver.

A Ride Down the Road ©2019

"I don't mean to make you nervous," James encouraged, "they will love you. Who wouldn't? You are warm and intelligent... you are beautiful... I don't mean to worry you. I'm sorry."

James squeezed her hand, rubbing his thumb over the top of her it. James' compliments always put her at ease. Hearing his praise and admiration was like food for her soul.

"So why do they push you so hard and put such heavy expectations on you?" Grace asked, breaking the silence. James frowned a bit and returned his hand to the steering wheel.

"Well, if I am to ever be president, then I need to be pushed. I need to understand how things really work, so that I can, one day, push things forward into a new era," James replied, almost as if he were reciting someone else's words.

"President?" Grace said with a smile, "You are already the bank president."

"No! President of the United States. I don't want to be just a bank president!" James said, staring straight forward and gripping the steering wheel a bit.

"*Just* a bank president*?*" Grace asked, reaching over and rubbing his arm. "It's a huge accomplishment to be a bank president. A lot of people would love to have a job like that plus it's an immense amount of responsibility."

"Grace, that kind of thinking will hold me back. I need you to be on board with this endeavor, you need to be supportive of my goals and ambitions. Especially in front of my parents." James directed.

Grace was confused. "Of course, dear," she said quietly. "I would always support your dreams. I just don't want you to think less of yourself. I don't want you to discount your many accomplishments."

They continued down the road discussing the politics of the day. Grace enjoyed listening to James and his ideas. He did most of the talking, often correcting her ideas and thoughts with ones he considered more prudent. He reminded her often of her lack of understanding of politics. Grace wanted to him to feel supported by her, but she also wanted him to support her having her own opinions. Yet she often was dismissed by James' assertions. She didn't like to be reminded of her 'place,' but, at the same time, didn't want to disappoint him. She also wasn't sure if this new piece of information about his ambitions to be "THE president" was something she was ready for, but she filed her fears away to pull out at a better time.

Storm clouds rolled in quickly and the skies opened. Sheets of rain fell on the car so hard that they couldn't see in front of them. James spotted a diner attached to a motel and pulled in. As they ran towards it, they got soaking wet, joining a host of other wet travelers who had stopped to get out of the chaos. They settled into a booth, and James ordered "the special" for both of them: pot roast, mashed potatoes, and a bottle of coke. They ate and watched as the rain poured down on the streets, filling the edges with large streams of water. James' ordered a piece of apple pie with whipped cream for them to share as they sipped their coffee.

The local sheriff walked into the diner and up to the café bar. He ordered a coffee, then turned and informed all the soggy travelers that the road was out ahead with no passage until at least the next day, maybe longer. Grace was concerned, they had already driven for half a day, and to turn back now would make them miss the upcoming event completely.

"Should we turn back?" Grace asked, setting her fork on the edge of the jadeite pie plate.

"No, of course not." James began running his fork along the plate to grab the last few morsels of pie. "We will just stay here tonight and leave in the morning."

"I… uh…" she stuttered, not sure how to respond to the proposition of staying in a motel.

"Don't worry. I will get you your own room." James smiled confidently as he rose from the table. "Wait here. I need to make a phone call, and then I'll take care of the arrangements."

He headed to a pay phone in the corner to call his parents and let them know of the delay. She heard a few words as he described the situation and responded to their questions. Then, he disappeared through a back door for a long time, eventually returning with 2 keys. He handed her one and explained how she could walk through the back door of the diner into the hotel office and that he would pull the car around and meet her there. She nodded and followed his directions.

When she made it to the front of the hotel, she waited patiently for James, watching as he parked the car and unloaded the suitcases. He ran between the raindrops to where she was standing, then they walked together under the covered walkway that led to her room. He unlocked the door and lead her in. She stood there surveying the room for a long moment, holding her suitcase with both hands.

"I will be back to check on you after I drop my things off," he said, leaning over and kissing her on top of her head.

"Ok," she replied nervously, as he left and closed the door behind him. She looked around her room, taking note of her surroundings. For furniture, there was a full size bed with a blue quilt and a small table with two chairs. On the wall hung a single picture: a paint-by-numbers image of a forest, stream and a bear. She liked the colors and stared at it for a while until she realized she was still standing in the entryway with her suitcase. She set it on the table and pulled out her nightgown and robe. The room felt empty. She was not used to being alone in a strange place, and the silence made her uncomfortable. She waited for several minutes, wondering if James was coming back to check on her.

A Ride Down the Road ©2019

"Maybe he forgot," she thought, as she walked around the room to inspect the bathroom and then the bedding. After a while, Grace decided that she should get ready for bed and try to get some rest.

"Perhaps he had a phone call or other business to attend too," she thought trying to comforted herself, slipping on her nightgown and reaching to fluff her pillow. The knock at the door startled her, but she soon heard James' familiar voice assuring her it was him. She quickly threw on her robe and cracked open the door.

"I've already put on my nightgown," she said, peeking through the door and smiling at her handsome boyfriend through the crack.

"Let me come in and make sure you are settled. It's ok. I am sure I will see you in a nightgown soon enough" he said with a wink. Conflicted, she sheepishly opened the door to let him in. He quickly looked the room over to make sure everything was as it should be, then turned and closed the door behind him. He checked the window to make sure it was locked, and even opened the closet door to make sure it was empty. Then, he turned to her, and they stared at each other for what felt like an eternity.

"Marry me," he said, taking her hand and pulling her in for a kiss. "Be my wife."

Neither statement was a request but rather a command. Grace was overwhelmed. He had talked of marriage before, but usually after a few drinks and always in a phrase that included "someday". His level of intoxication in those moments always made her question whether he was really in the right mind to ask.

"What?" she asked, wrapping her arms around his neck and accepting his kiss. She knew it was wrong to have a man in her room and most certainly wrong to *kiss* a man in her room. But she didn't want to be alone tonight in a strange place, away from home. The situation made Grace question

A Ride Down the Road ©2019

the right and wrong of it all, but that was nothing new she had been questioning *that* for weeks. She often wondered how long he would be patient with her avoidance of his advances. She did love him, but she was not sure love had to be translated into the physical ways he was always pushing for.

"Grace, will you marry me?" he asked, staring into her eyes. She believed him this time. There was truth behind his question instead of the usual playfulness. "I need you to make me a happy man, say yes!"

"Yes!" she said, laughing. Her dream was coming true: she would be married, have a family and finally *belong*. "Of course, I would love to marry you! I'd love to be your wife!"

With her "yes," James pursued her more passionately than before, and this time, caught up in the euphoria of the moment, Grace gave up… and gave in.

~ Chapter 12 ~

Lucy sat on the front porch thinking through the last few days. Senior year… parents getting divorced… wanting to stay in a nowhere town instead of going home...

She watched the clouds float carelessly across the sky and birds eat from her grandma's bird feeder. A bright red cardinal flew in and landed on a branch in the tree. She surveyed the branches for its mate. Soon, she spotted the tan bird and sighed. Grandma always said that it was good luck to see a male *and* female cardinal, a sign from above. The screen door opened with a creek. Grandma emerged, carrying a small tray with lemonade and cookies.

"Dear, I know all of this must be hard," Grandma started, as she sat the tray on the table and handed her granddaughter a glass, "But there is always a plan… God always has a plan, even when we humans try to mess things up. All things work together for good… all things, good *and* bad work together for God's ultimate good."

"Grandma, I love you, but I am starting to wonder what God is thinking… I mean, why all this? Why now? It makes me even wonder about *God*." Lucy reasoned.

"Dear, you know that, in *all* situations, we can see God… even the bad ones... even the ones where we don't feel Him. We know He is there." Grandma continued.

"I don't know how He in all this…" Lucy replied, sipping her lemonade. "Grandma, I want to stay with you this year. I want to stay here and finish up my school here."

"Are you running from your reality?" Grandma asked, setting her glass on the end table next to her chair. "Sometimes, God just wants us to go through a fire so that we can be better on the other side. Don't get me wrong, dear… I am old and would love a companion over the next year. I am not sure how much longer your mother will let me stay out here all alone. Remember, this is just a season. Seasons come

A Ride Down the Road ©2019

and go... some change quickly and some change slowly over time."

"What do you mean?" Lucy asked.

"Well, we all have winters where there seems to be no hope at all, all is dead and gone. It's cold and harsh. But spring comes after that season, and flowers start to push through the soil, trees start to bud with new life. Summer is a time of fun and relaxation but also a time of growth. Then comes the fall, a time of harvest of the work from before the time of a radiant passing," Grandma said, looking out over her tree. Lucy imagined what the tree would look like in each season. She had only ever seen it in summer, when the leaves were full.

"Let's just pray about it and see," advised Grandma.

Lucy knew that it would be difficult to transfer her senior year and difficult to leave her friends behind, but her friends would all be leaving at the end of next year anyway, so what was a few months early? She didn't want to experience the back and forth. She didn't want to live through her parents living their own lives instead of a life together. So much change in such a short period of time... was this her fall, or would this be her spring?

They sat and talked on the porch for hours, then went in the house and made dinner together. The kitchen was filled with laughter as Lucy tried to learn how to make chicken and homemade dumplings. She had managed to get flour in her hair, as well as all over the counters and floor. Grandma was not pleased with the mess, but she was certainly pleased with the joy.

"I haven't been this happy in a long time," Grandma told her, as they held hands to bless their food that night. "I would love for you to stay this year, dear... but I am not sure if that's what God wants. I always want what He wants. It makes life easier."

A Ride Down the Road ©2019

They cleaned up after dinner, then went on to bed. As she did each night, she pulled out the journal and began to read.

I gave in to James' advances. He wants to marry me. I want to marry him. I know it's not ok. I know it's not what I should do, but I want to make him happy. I woke up today wondering if I made a mistake. He was asleep in the bed next to me, which was nice, but somehow, I still feel strangely alone. This was wrong, but felt right… We will hopefully get on our way to Jefferson City today. I hope that it all goes well this week.

Grace quietly got out of bed, collected her clothes from the suitcase, and went to the bathroom to get ready. She showered, then wiped the foggy mirror to see her face. Staring back at her was a face of question and worry. *What had she done?!* She got dressed, then walked back into the room to find James gone. Fear shot through her body as she stood alone in the motel room. The quilt was strewn across the unmade bed. She wondered if he would return, then scolded herself for even thinking that. She took a deep breath and began to pack her things in her suitcase, then busied herself with tidying up the room. As she was straightening the bedding, she spotted a note on her pillow.
Be back soon. Went to get dressed. I love you. -- James

Relieved, she picked up the note and sat on the bed, staring out the window.   He soon arrived, and they loaded up the car, smiling at one another, James leaning in every now and then for a quick kiss.   They held hands as they ate breakfast at the diner. He ordered her eggs and bacon with toast – same as him. James went to the office to make sure the road was open, and they went on their way. In the car, they held hands again and chatted about children and the future.

"I would like to get married at the church that Christopher preaches at," Grace said excitedly, painting a picture in her head of the beautiful day. The congregation would smile as they watched her walk down the aisle in a beautiful white dress. Her bouquet of colorful flowers would be wrapped

A Ride Down the Road ©2019

with a soft satin ribbon. Laura would be standing there next to her in an elegant blue dress.

"You're cute! But that won't be possible," James laughed. "We have to get married at the cathedral my parents attend. It will be grand, with all I of the 'who's who' in attendance. Christopher can attend, but we'll get a more well-known priest to do the actual service."

"But I'm not Catholic," she protested weakly, not sure if he was really being serious. "How would I get married in a Catholic service?"

"It's not a problem, you can convert," he stated matter-of-factly. "It will be fine."

Grace was silent. She realized that he wasn't joking at all, so she tried to pick her words carefully. She was sure he would understand where she was coming from, she just had to help him understand. He did say he loved her, after all.

"James, I don't... *want* to convert. Why would I have to be the one to change? You don't even *attend* church, or at least not regularly." As she said the words out loud, she felt a twinge inside as Laura's question came to the forefront of her mind: *Does he help point you to Jesus?*

James tone changed a bit as he shot back, "I don't see why it's such a big deal, Grace. It doesn't really matter, it's just a ceremony filled with traditional things… we just need to do what's expected of us…we can believe or attend whatever and wherever we want later."

"But, James, I think it *does* matter. Christopher says that a union between two people is actually a triune. There is a third person in the relationship and that's Jesus… We need to have a service that represents that truth, and it needs to be performed by someone we know and trust." Grace stated uncomfortably realizing that her actions the night before didn't represent a thing she was saying.

James sighed and looked frustrated. "We can figure it out later… it's not important for today. Let's not bring it up to my parents this week, what with them just meeting you and all... I don't want to cause a stir."

Grace nodded meekly, unsure of what to do or say. She was sure she did not want to pretend to join the Catholic church just to have a ceremony in their building. She was also sure she didn't want to disappoint James or create a problem with his parents. But she was *not* sure how to answer any of his parents' questions about their engagement or future plans.

"Once I am elected Senator, we will move to Washington DC," James began, holding his hand out as if to motion East towards their new home.

"Move to DC?!" interrupted Grace, surprised by the idea. She had imagined that a move to Springfield might be in order but had hoped to find a way to somehow fulfill her commitment to teach, at least through the end of the year.

"Yes, we'll move, of course! We will be going to Washington DC once I am elected so that I can serve in the Senate and get experience to become president," he continued, his jaw starting to tighten as they drove towards his parents' house.

"James, if you become Senator, then we can most certainly *talk* about it," Grace said in a tone she had never used with him before. She was polite yet very direct with her words. "I thought you were kidding with all of that yesterday. The idea of becoming President."

"Idea!?" James replied indignantly. "Don't talk like that. I need full commitment and someone who believes that I WILL win!"

"Yes, of course you could win," she started, trying to assure him, but he sharply cut her off.

A Ride Down the Road ©2019

"Stop it!" he commanded, his voice angry, "*Could and if* will not be part of our vocabulary over the next few years. *WHEN* and *WILL* are going to be the words we use… nothing else."

Grace paused and took a deep breath. She was taken aback by his tone of voice and knew that she had to respond wisely. "I'm sorry," she said, "WHEN you win, will you move there? And then what will that mean for *us*?"

"Well, it means you will move to DC with me. We will get married, then move to DC," he stated, leaving no room for opposition. Grace realized that he had decided long ago how things would go but must have never felt the need to share his plans for the two of them… with her.

"Move *with* you?" she asked, rubbing her hands together nervously. "But my school... and the commitment to the town... They are *counting* on me and Laura is counting on me."

"You don't need to worry about work… there are not enough people in that little town to count, anyway. Don't worry, I don't need *their* votes to win," James laughed scornfully, changing lanes to pass a slow moving car. He kept increasing his speed.

"I wasn't talking about you needing them to win!" she replied incredulously. "I was talking about how they are paying for my college so that I can come back and be their teacher. Those are good people, and I want to be good on my word. At least for a year or so… at least till I can help them find someone to take my place. At that point, maybe I can pay them back for some of the college cost."

"Listen," James replied curtly, "If we are getting married, then this is an _us_ thing. My parents will expect *us* to be on board with it. They expect you and I to be focused on the end goal. You won't be teaching once I get to the senate… and you won't be teaching at *all* once we are married. What would people think if my wife worked?" James asked. The more agitated he became, the more the speed of the car seemed to increase.

"But James, a lot of people work, and, these days, a lot of women teach! We won't have children right away, so I could at least work for a while…" Grace said, reaching over to rub his arm. "James," she said again, trying to settle him, "I just think we should talk to each other about things that involve in our future. It's my *dream* to be something more than what I am today to have an education and teach children."

Suddenly, James slammed on the breaks and pulled the car to the side of the road. Not sure of what was happening, Grace had to brace herself in the car as she let out a cry of fear. As soon as the car stopped, he threw it into park and quickly grabbed her by the shoulders.

"*My* future includes the senate and the presidency...*my* future is decided, and if you don't want to be part of it, then you need to let me know *now*. I am not going to tolerate any more of this disagreement. You will be on board with this, and what I say goes! Do you understand?!"

Grace was terrified by his increasingly hostile tone. "I am sorry," she heard herself saying over and over as his grip on her shoulders tightened. She winced as his fingers dug into her arms. "James, please," she said. "You are hurting me. *Please*."

James released her shoulders, seeming surprised by his own rage. He turned away from her and put his hands back on the steering wheel. They sat in silence as the cars on the road buzzed by.

"I am just worried about leaving my home," Grace said, looking over at him warily, slightly afraid of his reaction. "But what *was* that… what just happened?" she asked slowly, rubbing her arms and trying to catch her breath.

"The sooner you realize that place is not your home, the better your life will be," James said coldly, "Those people are

A Ride Down the Road ©2019

not your family. They are just people who took in a penniless orphan. A pastor is practically required by occupation to do those sorts of things."

His words hurt her now more than his angry outburst from a few minutes earlier. He knew that her one desire was to have a family and a home. He knew that Laura and Christopher had said over and over that they were her family that this was her home. She sat staring at him, unsure of what to say and regretting more and more the night before. She was unable to stop the tears from rolling down her cheeks. She turned from him and looked out the window at the wet landscape.

"I am not an orphan anymore, I have a family..." she whispered to the window, letting her forehead rest against it.

"Face the facts," he said, reaching over and touching her shoulder, "You are blessed by the generosity of someone who is required by their profession to be generous. They have their own family now and a new baby. It's too much to ask to be in their home and constantly in their way."

Grace looked over at him. The anger was gone, and he seemed to be back to normal. She nodded, not really agreeing, but wanting the argument to stop. James pulled the car back on to the road and started driving.

"But don't worry, that's all going to change for you," James said, reaching over and holding her hand. "You have *me* now. We will be married, and *we* will be a family. This is a dream come true for or a girl in your situation. It's what you have always wanted, right? To have a family?"

"Yes," she replied. As they drove down the road, her mind began to wander back to the days at the house with three gables and to their happy times around the table. Smiling, laughing, talking, and eating with people who cared about her. Laura's smiling assurances, Christopher's strong protection, the church members kindness... David's words "we are family" were echoing in her head. No one had ever

A Ride Down the Road ©2019

made her feel anything less than loved in that group of people that she called a family. She had come to accept that families don't always look like some picture book. That they come in different forms and have different functions. She knew that they loved her and that they cared for her, no matter what James said.

The rest of the ride was very quiet, and any conversation centered around the weather or the scenery. Grace was uneasy, confused, and searching her brain for answers she could not find.

~ Chapter 13 ~

The green pickup truck was sitting in the driveway of the farmhouse when Lucy wandered out on the porch with her biscuit. Grandma had left her a large plate of them, along with pork sausage gravy and even eggs. Lucy didn't notice the truck until she was seated on the swing, and she froze as she realized that she was in her Justice League pajama pants and t-shirt. Her hair was a messy mop, tied back in a low bun. She looked around frantically as she jumped up and ran inside with her plate, right at the moment that Tucker walked in through the back door.

"Good morning!" he said cheerily, enjoying the face that he caught her off-guard. "Just waking up?" He reached for a plate and grabbed a biscuit.

Grandma, who was right behind him, was carrying a bucket of blackberries. "Lucy!" she called out excitedly, "Look what Tucker brought us, it's enough for a pie! I'll get them cleaned up and ready to go."

She eyed her granddaughter, who stood holding her plate in the family room, "What are you doing in there? You look like a deer in the headlights! Come in here and eat with us, *dear*," Grandma said, as she laughed and put the bucket in the sink.

Lucy quickly went to her seat, not saying a word. Tucker hung his hat on the hat rack by the door. Lucy had never noticed before, but now she saw that there was a man's flannel jacket hanging on the hook. On top of the jacket was an old cap with plastic, mesh sides. It was dirty and had a BNSF railroad sign on it. It must have been her grandpa's. Tucker joined her at the table, grinning the whole time. He was delighted to make her blush a little.

"Grandma asked if I would come check the fence line today. Want to take a ride with me and check things out?"

A Ride Down the Road ©2019

Lucy nodded, trying not to make eye contact. She hoped that her naked face didn't have mascara smeared on her cheek since she fell asleep reading the letters last night. Worse, her messy bun wasn't the fancy kind, it was more of the "bed head" variety. She was mortified.

"Lucy, Tucker was telling me there is a picnic at the church tomorrow night. I think we should go. Wouldn't that be nice?" Grandma asked, filling her plate. Lucy replied with a nod and quickly finished her breakfast.

"I'll go change," said Lucy, jumping up from the table and hurrying back down the hallway.

"What for?" Tucker asked, chuckling a bit, then calling over his shoulder, "You look like you could take on the whole universe."

"They were a gift..." Lucy called out, her voice trailing down the hallway, "and besides, I like superhero movies! And they're comfortable!"

In her room, she changed into jeans and one of her school t-shirts. Quickly fixing her hair and rushing to the bathroom to brush her teeth. When she returned, Tucker was standing by the door with a small cooler, talking to Grandma.

"I will have her home before midnight!" he said, as he opened the door for Lucy. They walked out to his truck.

"Ok, dear," Grandma said, smiling as she walked out on the small back stoop.

"Race ya!" Tucker said, taking off towards the truck with Lucy hot on his heels. They jumped in and took off for the field, chatting and carrying on as if they had known each other for years, not just weeks. Lucy found him easy to talk to and always willing to listen. He was never self-focused or sarcastic, and he always wanted to know what she thought.

A Ride Down the Road ©2019

Tucker found the truck ruts and drove along an existing path to the fence line.

"Pretty sure these have been here forever, or at least since your grandparents have been here," he said. "I always try to find them, it's so much easier. Like your grandpa cleared a path for us to help know where to go. If I drive through the field, there are holes and tree limbs. The ruts avoid all that."

They came up to a broken fence post, and he stopped the truck. "Well, *that* one will have to be fixed. Let's get to work."

"Work? How are we going to fix *that*?" Lucy asked, surprised that their joyride included manual labor.

"Well, we are going to use the stuff in the back of the truck to fix the fence," he said, grinning at her. "Come on, let's go, Princess."

He got out of the truck and she sat there for a minute.

Wait, did he just call me princess?! She thought then scrambled out after him. "Hey! I am *not* a princess!" she said, reaching into the tool box and pulling out a screw driver.

"Ok," he replied. "Well, we won't need a screwdriver on this one."

She threw it back into the tool bag and looked for something else. Tucker pulled out a board, hammer and some nails, then walked towards the fence.

"Are you coming?" he asked, as he dropped the board in the grass by the edge of the fence and put on his brown leather work gloves. Lucy watched as he pulled a pair of large wire cutters from his back pocket and cut the broken barbed wire at one end.

A Ride Down the Road ©2019

"You're going to want gloves," he advised, pulling the fence back out of the weeds. She went back to the truck and found a pair in his toolbox. They smelled sweaty, but she put them on anyway and went back to grab the barbed wire.

"Just put it by the truck for me. I'll put it in the back in a minute." She followed his instructions, then came back to wait for the next.

"Grab that end for me," he said, as he picked up the long piece of wood. She steadied it while he pulled a nail from the side of his ball cap and began hammering his end into the post.

"A fence is an interesting thing. It's made to keep things in... but also to keep things out. This is just a patch for now."

Lucy looked at the fence and thought about what she read the night before in the journals. James' family certainly had a fence around their family and a plan on who would be in and who would be out.

The governor's mansion is incredible. It's a large brick home with a beautiful fence around it. It is grand, with large windows and a stately porch. We arrived mid-day and were greeted by James' mother.   His father was busy with his duties. She took us on a tour of the first floor as the servants put our things in our rooms.

"This is our parlor," James' mother, Judith, said, as they walked into a beautifully appointed room. The ceilings were high, with a majestic chandelier in the middle of the room. There were magnificent sitting areas with ornate furniture, and a stately fireplace. Judith reminded Grace of the women who would come to see her mother's shows: Women with fine clothes, deliberate movements, and... a critical eye.

Grace was almost afraid to touch anything, and suddenly felt underdressed just to be in the room.   She caught a glance of herself in the mirror and quickly smoothed her hair.

A Ride Down the Road ©2019

"Would you like to go freshen up, dear?" Judith asked, noticing Grace's movement. "You look a bit weathered from the journey. I should have asked before we started."

"Oh," she replied, embarrassed. "Yes, would you mind?"

"The hotel you stayed at must have been… quaint," Judith continued, raising her eyebrow a bit at the plainly dressed girl. It seemed as if Judith was judging Grace's every move.

"It was very nice," Grace replied, wondering if his mother suspected any indiscretion. Her face felt hot as her cheeks flushed. She looked at James for support, but he had walked to the other end of the room.

"Anita!" Judith said sharply, turning from Grace and clapping her hands a bit. A young girl showed up dressed in a simple black dress with a long white apron.

"Yes, Ms." she reported, standing straight and still. Judith walked over to her and straightened her collar.

"Ms. McCombs would like to go freshen up. Take her to her room," Judith said sternly, as she turned and faced Grace.

Grace followed Anita out of the room, and as they walked up the stairs, she overheard Judith say to James, "*That* is the best you could do? She is…"

Grace stopped in horror and peeked through the corridor at James and Judith.

"*Beautiful*," James said, as he completed her sentence. He laughed, walking towards his mother, "Like a penny that needs shining, Mother. Give her a chance."

"That would be a lot of scrubbing," Judith said, shaking her head and walking away.

Grace continued following Anita to her room. "Had she already made a bad impression?" she wondered.

Her room was very formal, with a large four-post bed and beautiful chenille bedding. Grace entered slowly; her eyes wide. Beautiful paintings covered the walls. A large walnut Eastlake wardrobe with carved handles and an ornate top sat next to the bed. Grace ran her hand along the wood-paneled doors.

"There is a bathroom through that door. Would you like me to draw your bath?" Anita asked, as she started towards the bathroom. Then she hesitated, eyeing Grace innocently. "You are different than the other girls he's dated before…"

"Oh? How so?" Grace asked, looking out the large window at the trees. They all still seemed dead though spring should have arrived already.

"I probably shouldn't say anything," Anita replied.

"It's ok, I won't be offended," Grace said, turning to her.

"Well, Miss… You look like one of *us*. Not one of them." With that, Anita left and went into the bathroom to draw the bath.

Hours later Grace stood in front of a mirror wearing the dress that James bought for her. It was red and form-fitting. Anita had assisted her with her hair and makeup. Grace wasn't confident in her ability to do it herself. The two chatted like old friends about where Anita was raised and how she ended up in the governor's mansion. She was an orphan, like Grace, who had been taken in by a local family, people she referred to as her "keepers". She had not been permitted to finish high school as she needed to find work to help her keepers. She had worked for the previous governor and felt like this was as much her home as the new tenants'.

"They all leave, you know. Serving as the governor is just for a period of time, not a lifetime, like some may want," Anita said, as she carefully put a broach in Grace's hair.

A Ride Down the Road ©2019

"Ms. Grace, are you ready?" She put her hand on Grace's shoulder.

"Ready as I will ever be I suppose," Grace replied, smiling at herself in the mirror. She had never looked so done up. "Do you think that I will fit in?" she asked.

"Honestly, no, ma'am," Anita replied. "No offense, but I don't think you were made to fit in with these people. Really, you wouldn't want to."

"Thank you for your help," Grace said, hugging her new friend, not sure what else to say. Then she left the room to go to the dinner.

As Grace walked down the stairs, she was greeted by a tuxedo-clad James. He looked like Rhet Butler as he leaned against the railing. He smiled as he took her hand.

"You look amazing! Perfect, even! It's almost time for dinner," he said, guiding her into the parlor where a small group of people were gathered. They were talking and drinking, but everyone stopped and stared as the couple entered the room.

"Everyone," James said, "This is Grace! Grace, this is everyone."

The room was silent. Grace felt like a million eyes were examining her and searching for flaws. She knew she should stop thinking that way, but James' words kept echoing in her head about fitting in. The women, dripping in jewelry, were dressed in the finest dresses, and they eyed her keenly.

"Welcome, Grace. We are glad you could join us." A sizable dark-haired man walked from the side of the room towards Grace and James, his hand extended, "I am Governor Henry Carter."

Grace smiled and clung tightly to James' arm. "Hello, Governor Carter."

"Please, call me 'Henry'," he insisted, taking Grace's hand and kissing it. "We are glad to finally meet you. James has been telling us all about the beautiful girl from Springfield that he has been so taken by."

The crowd soon returned to their small talk, several looking over at Grace as she spoke with the governor. Her hands would normally be shaking from nerves, but she kept one tucked in James' arm and the other close to her side. The governor kept the conversation light, sticking mostly to the weather and news about the town.

"Are you excited about the run for office?" Judith asked, as she walked to her husband's side. Grace wondered if it was obvious how uncomfortable she felt.

"Yes, of course," Grace replied, trying to appear as poised as possible, what with James' earlier admonitions to "try to blend in." Not wanting them to question her support for their son's political ambitions, she added, "James will be an outstanding Senator."

Judith raised an eyebrow as she stated, "Your family must be excited to know that their daughter is dating a soon-to-be senator. What have your parents said about the upcoming campaign?" Grace hesitated, not knowing how to respond.

James quickly jumped in to assist her, "They are pleased! More than pleased!" Then he added, "Her father even committed a campaign contribution all ready."

Grace was shocked and not sure how to respond. She managed to look up at James with a weak smile, and he beamed back down at her.

"Mother, didn't you say it's time for dinner soon?" James asked. Grace could tell he was trying to change the subject,

A Ride Down the Road ©2019

which she appreciated, but she was completely dumbfounded by the lie about her father.

Judith looked at the door and nodded at the servant. "We are ready for dinner. Let the staff know." The servant nodded and left the room. Judith motioned to the dining room, calling the group to come enjoy some dinner. As people started to walk to the room, Grace paused and pulled at James lightly. He stopped and whispered in her ear, "I will explain later. Just go with it... I want you to fit in." The he kissed her forehead lightly.

"Explain later" she thought, "What was there to explain? It was a complete *lie*."

She had only just found out about the campaign. They had certainly not mentioned anything to her family, let alone her to her father, who didn't exist! She took a deep breath and walked with James.

The dining room table was fitting for such a stately house and stately company: It was adorned with beautiful, white china that was crested with an eagle and flag. The dishes were flanked on each side with perfectly polished silverware. Candles lined the center of the table on crystal stands. Small vases of white flowers were placed evenly between the candles on the bright red runner.

James sat to the left of the governor, with Grace next to him. Across from her, next to Judith, was a beautiful blonde-haired woman wearing a revealing black dress. She was perfectly put together, her hair pinned back with a jeweled flower and her makeup flawless. She kept whispering to Judith, and they would both laugh quietly, often looking over at Grace.

Grace ate quietly and listened to the varied conversations. Politics... society... people she had never heard of, doing things that they disapproved of, all for saving face with those in their circle. It was a constant stream of judgmental statements, each one comparing their achievements with the

A Ride Down the Road ©2019

others'. The low rumble of conversation was only interrupted by the occasional comments of the governor.   When the governor spoke, the room would get quiet, but then they'd pick up steam and jump back into their comparisons and judgments.

"Grace," the blonde said, staring at James. "Tell us about your father's business. James said he was very successful."

James stopped eating and glared at the blonde. Grace was unsure what to do, as being truthful would make for poor and suddenly complicated dinner conversation.   She looked helplessly at James. He took a bite of his dinner and didn't make eye contact. She was stuck… she either had to lie or embarrass James and his family.

"I suppose you could call it 'successful'," Grace replied, as the room grew quiet and all eyes locked on her. Grace blushed, desperately wishing James would speak up. "But we are in a room filled with successful people, so that's nothing new to any of you."

"James told me that your father was very excited about the campaign and would be sure to visit soon. I am sure Judith and Henry would *love* to meet him," the blonde continued, smiling slyly. Grace nodded, out of words as she thought to herself, "I'd sure like to meet him, as well…"

"Grace, tell us about your classes," Judith continued, as she sipped her wine.

Finally, there was a topic Grace that felt comfortable discussing.

"Well, they are rigorous, but I enjoy the challenge. It's exciting, really," Grace answered, setting down her fork. "I am thankful for the opportunity to be there, really. Not everyone gets the chance to go to college. I hope that my education will benefit my town."

A Ride Down the Road ©2019

"So, you plan to go home to New York when you are finished?" the blonde said shrewdly, as she raised her brow with a little smirk.

"No, I'll be going back to Radical, it's just south of Springfield." As soon as Grace said it, she wished she could pull back her words.

"I see. The college has already chosen your placement?" Judith asked, her brow wrinkled with confusion. Grace was not sure what to say. Again, she looked over at James for help, but he sat there, silent, and continued to eat.

"No, my family lives there," she managed to say.

"But I thought they were from New York?" the blonde shot back, smiling in a way that made Grace wonder what she knew and if there was a reason she was pushing so hard. It seemed as though she was simply trying to bait her.

"My cousin and her husband live in Radical," Grace started hesitantly, then continued, "I live with them now." James reached over and grabbed her hand.

"She means on breaks," James interjected. "She stays with them when she's on break."

Dinner went on and Grace kept quiet. She listened as the governor told the group of his triumphs while in office and his plans for future progress Many talked about the lake and its benefits to the Springfield area: How wonderful a lake would be, and how the visitors would bring in needed revenue. After dinner, the visitors began to trickle out of the room to retrieve their coats and head home. Grace watched as the beautiful blonde extended her hand for James to kiss. Something did not seem right.

After the crowd left, Grace made her way to the back porch to get some fresh air. The sky was clear and the stars sparkled like the women's fancy jewelry. The evening had been more overwhelming than she expected. How did something that seemed to be what she always dreamed of now seem so troubling? She always imagined that the people in her mother's audiences, the ones she grew up watching from the side of the stage, had happy exciting lives. That their evenings were filled with fancy meals and exciting conversations. Tonight, the meal was delicious, but the people seemed consumed with how they compared to others. Especially James. She couldn't even comprehend why he would lie about her family. Was it just to appear more powerful? The entire evening was a disappointment. It didn't feel at all like she thought it would feel.

"What are you doing out here?" James asked, walking up behind her and wrapping his arms around her. "You will freeze!"

She wiggled out of his arms and faced him. "Why did you lie to your family about me?" she demanded, crossing her arms tightly in front of her.

"I plan to tell my parents, but didn't think tonight was the best time or place… you know, in front of all of these people," he replied, holding his hands up defensively as if he were trying to brush away the truth.

"James, you lied to them about me and then left me to try to figure out how to answer!" Grace said, feeling her heart racing in her chest.

"I know you don't understand all of this… what it means to be part of society and how people talk. Where you are from and who your family is or is not it means something in my world," he said, leaning in closer to her.

"No, I *don't* know what it's like to lie to my family! And then expect someone I love to continue that lie! That's what you are asking me to do, but that's not who I am," she said, backing away from him. "I would *never* do that to you."

"You wouldn't have to!" he chuckled, as he moved towards here, backing her into the rail. "Grace, you are in the governor's mansion and just had dinner with the 'who's who' of this state. You can't walk in there and be *from* nothing, with no family, no connections, and expect people to respect you! You just don't understand."

"No, I don't understand," she said, gripping the rail behind her. She felt strong as she spoke, looking straight into his eyes.

"James." A deep voice came from behind him. They both turned to see the governor standing at the doorway. "Can I see you in my office…"

James sighed, shaking his head at her, disappointed. "Now look what you've done…"

Grace waited until he left, then turned to look at the night sky. She wished she could climb into the big dipper cup and fly away. She waited a moment longer, then quietly entered the house and walked towards the stairs. She heard muffled voices in the office near the stairs, so she tiptoed over to peek through the crack in the door. The governor stood behind his desk, both hands placed on it. "So she is not from New York?" the governor asked his son.

"Yes, she is from New York, but her parents are dead… well, her *mother* is dead. I'm not sure about her father. She lives with her cousin in Radical, Missouri. I was going to tell you all, but…"

"But what? You knew we would not approve!" the governor replied crisply. For a moment, Grace thought he would reprimand James for thinking he was that insensitive. After all, weren't politicians supposed to represent *all* people, *especially* the weak?

"Well, you were right," the governor continued, "You don't need someone like that at your side. What do you really know about this girl, anyway?"

A Ride Down the Road ©2019

"Dad, she is really a wonderful young woman," James said, walking over to the desk. "She is attending the University - she is smart, and -"

"James, you need to be serious about your future," the Governor cautioned, as he interrupted his son and walked around the desk. He put his arm around James as he continued, "Have your fun with her and then move on. You need to find a *real* partner for your run. Someone like her would not be helpful."

Grace stepped away from the door, horrified. "*Have your fun with her?*" she screamed in her head, quickly walking up the stairs and then into her room. All the fine things. All the beautiful bedding and artwork and furniture. All of the things she had dreamed of...what did they gain? Nothing. Nothing at all.

~ Chapter 14 ~

After dinner, Lucy, Grandma, and Tucker sat on the front porch with their blackberry pie and ice cream. The warm, purple liquid from the pie melted the ice cream and swirled in the bottom of Lucy's plate. Pieces of crust looked like shipwrecked vessels half submerged in the sea of sweetness.

"How bad were the fences?" Grandma asked, looking over at Tucker.

"You are going to have to have that barbed wire fixed next spring. I think it's on its last leg," Tucker replied, as he layered a large bite of pie and ice cream. Lucy smiled as she thought about how he was creating the perfect bite each time.

"Well… I knew that time would come, eventually… things don't last forever," Grandma replied with a sigh. "You know, we moved here because we outgrew the house with three gables. The kids were getting bigger and there were more of them. Your grandpa wanted to be closer to town for the kids to be able to get to school. He and David put that fence in. You can still see some of the original places where they used trees as posts," she said, staring off into the distance. "Thank you for patching it up, dear."

The three sat and talked about the fence, Lucy's repair adventures, and learning how to use tools. As the sun set, it cast jewel-toned color across the pasture, starkly contrasting with the fields in front of the house. Grandma stood and started to collect the plates.

"So where are you at in the journal?" Tucker asked, as he handed Grandma his plate and thanked her.

"Ummm… Grace just had dinner at the governor's mansion," she said, swirling her spoon to mix the melted ice cream with the juice from the pie. "It didn't seem to go well.

A Ride Down the Road ©2019

James is kind of a creep," Lucy said, scooping up her last bite and handing the plate to Grandma.

"'Creep' is a good description for him," Grandma said, shuddering at the memory. "Grace cried for days after that event. She didn't tell me the extent of everything for a long while, but I could tell how she was hurting."

"I don't understand how that family could reject her like that. I mean, aren't governors supposed to represent *all* the people?" Lucy asked, "Besides, surely Missouri didn't have a *lot* of wealthy people back then. Why did it matter that she was an orphan?"

"Wealth and image were everything to that family. At some point, James was probably just like all of us, looking for happiness, but he looked for it in the wrong way. He listened to the wrong people," Grandma replied. "He believed that having a beautiful girl on his arm made him appear successful. Having a successful career made him appear important. In some ways, that was a simpler time, but in others, the complexity of society and fitting in were harder."

Lucy nodded, then smiled at her grandma. She was beautiful. She still had a bright smile, and her hair was shimmering white. She was the last one of her friends and close family left living, besides her children. Lucy wondered if she felt lonely not having them all here to talk to and enjoy. Grandma mentioned several times how nice it will be to see them all again soon, because "death isn't 'goodbye' it's only 'see ya later'."

"I am going to bed. I know I didn't work like you two, but this old bird needs her beauty rest. Lucy, leave the dishes in the sink, we will get them in the morning," Grandmas said, opening the door to head to bed.

"Wait, Grandma!" Tucker said, jumping to his feet and hurrying over to give her a hug. She tapped his shoulder and he leaned down so she could kiss the top of his head.

"Just like when you were little, you came to find me each Sunday to get your kiss," Grandma said, patting his cheek as she left.

"I better get going, too," Tucker said, stretching his arms up where his fingertips could touch the ceiling of the porch.

"Are you sure?" she asked, hoping that he would change his mind and stay longer.

"Yeah, I have practice in the morning and need my beauty rest, too," he replied, laughing and skipping down the front steps. Lucy quickly walked to the edge of the porch and hung on the post as he did a little jig on the walkway.

"Thanks for today," Lucy said.

"What? For working you in a hot field all day with no pay? You... are... welcome," he laughed, running his hand through his hair.

"No, I mean all of the time you have been spending with me. It has helped," she replied, hugging the porch post.

"Listen," Tucker said, as he stopped dancing. "You need a friend right now. I remember what it's like, and I am glad to be that friend."

"Friends are good. Thanks," she replied.

"I gotta go. Maybe you and Grandma can come see my game this week?" he asked, as he turned to walk to his truck. "I am one heck of a pitcher... and sooo humble."

"That would be great!" Lucy replied. She watched him as he climbed into the truck and drove onto the street. He stuck his hat out the window to wave.

"See you at the game! Remember to wear red!" he called. Lucy laughed as she went inside. She grabbed her knapsack off the table and found the journals and letters.

A Ride Down the Road ©2019

She decided that the couch would be the best option tonight and curled up with an orange, green, and brown afghan.

Graduation day. I am glad to be done and glad to go back home. It's been more than a week since I heard from James. He told me he would not be at the ceremony because he needed to go to Saint Louis for a campaign event last week. No letters or calls to the dorm since he left. I am sure that he is busy....

After the ceremony, Grace was joyfully greeted by Laura, the baby, and Christopher. She hugged her dear cousin and examined her soft little bundle. The baby was wrapped in a tiny quilt with kitten applique stitched on to white blocks. One kitten was playing with yarn the other one sleeping, curled up in a ground ball... both blissfully unaware of the world around them.

"He has grown so much!" Grace said, gently touching his thick, curly hair, black like his father's.

"We are proud of you!" Laura said, kissing her cousin's cheek. "This is quite an accomplishment, and we are so excited about what God will do with your future! With this teaching certificate, you will be able to help so many people!"

David and the boys emerged from the building, and Albert took off running for Grace as soon as he saw her.

"GRAAAAACEE!" he yelled, as he ran and flung himself at her, his enthusiasm almost knocking her to the ground. His red curls were longer and his face fuller than the last time she saw him. He buried his face in her skirt.

"Albert!" David said, hurrying behind him. "Softly, remember? *Soft* touches. She's a girl!" he shrugged regrettably at Grace, "Sorry... we have been working on that, but it has obviously not sunk in yet. Last week at church, he knocked over Mrs. Shaver with his overly excited hug.

Grace knelt, taking Albert's face in her hands. "You've grown! Look at you!" she said, her eyes welling up with tears. "I have missed so much! You are practically a grown-up."

"Look," he said, opening his mouth. "I lost a tooth and am getting a new one."

Grace hugged him close. "I hate that I missed all of that excitement, sweet boy."

Ben muscled his way in for his hug next and delighted her with stories of the farm. He played with her hair as he talked to her. As she stood, each boy slipped their hand in one of hers, and she grinned at David.

"Congratulations," he said, his blue eyes shining. "Clearly, we are *all* glad that you will be home soon."

Home. It sounded good to Grace. Her home and her family. She watched as they all continued to chatter on about the people from home, the town preparing to change its name, and the coming lake. The happiness she felt warmed her like a beam of sunshine on a cool day.

"Here, let me take a picture of you with my new camera," said Laura, pulling a Brownie box camera from the car. Carefully, she turned the crank and held it at her waist, framing up the picture of her family. Grace, David, Christopher, and the children gathered in front of the school. David threw his arm around Grace's shoulders, and Christopher stepped in close, holding the baby with one arm. The boys stood in front, with Albert holding tightly to Grace's skirt and Ben holding her hand.

"3-2-1!" Laura counted down.

The afternoon continued with packing up her things and putting them in the back of David's truck, green as the grass in the meadows. It was a welcome sight. What wasn't as welcome to her sight was the dress she wore to the dinner with the Carters. It was hanging in a store cover with a zipper front. She looked at it briefly, then folded it over and laid it in the bed of the truck.

"Do you want to bring that in the cab?" David asked, eyeing the bag. "It looks expensive… are you sure you want it in the back of the truck?"

"Its fine. It's not important," she said, laying her suitcase on top of it. David nodded and continued to pack, not questioning her about it again. As they finished, she turned and stared at the college. It was a grand stone edifice of higher education. The columns in the front made it look like a courthouse and not a college. Grace sighed at the thought of it. The educators inside were like judges of your abilities, your worthiness to teach youth.

"How many women get to go to a place like this and gain the knowledge I've gained?" she said to herself. "To be educated itself is a gift. Regardless of who actually paid the bill, it was a gift from God to get to go here, and a gift should never be taken advantage of or tossed aside." She felt tears well up inside her as she wondered if she had squandered her gift already, if she had failed the test. Was she even worthy of such a gift?

"Grace," David said, interrupting her inner monologue, "It's time to go home."

They loaded the boys, beyond excited, in the jump seat of the Nash. Grace and David climbed into the cab of the green truck.

"Are you ready?" he asked, as he put the truck into gear and drove away from the school. Grace looked over at the college for a moment, then back at her friend. She realized that one chapter was closing but she was hopeful for a new one to begin.

"Yes, I want to go home," she said, looking out the windshield and down the road ahead.

They drove through the streets of the busy town. Cars were parked on either side. A Texaco light glowed in front of them and people were hustling down the streets with boxes and bags from their shopping adventures. Men passed by in suits with formal hats, and women hobbled by in heeled shoes with calf-length skirts.

"Where was James today?" David asked, as he turned the corner onto 13 Highway to head South. The road became a little rougher the farther they went from town.

"He had a campaign meeting in St. Louis," she replied, looking out the window. The ground was starting to come alive after the winter freeze. Green grass peeked out from the brown earth and dead tree limbs were starting to regenerate with little sparks of new leaves. Spring was coming, proof that God makes all things new.

"Is he helping with his father's re-election?" David asked, looking over to see Grace wringing her hands uncomfortably.

"No…" she started, looking out the window then down at her hands and remembering James' admonishing her that it wasn't a matter of "if" but "when." She stopped and took a deep breath as she replied, "he is running for Senate. He's working on his *own* campaign."

"Senate? The US Senate in Washington, DC?" David said in disbelief. He paused for a minute as it sunk in, then asked nervously, "What does it mean for you?"

There was silence in the cab as Grace considered her words and tried to keep herself composed. She looked at her hands and then smoothed the wrinkles from her skirt.

"He asked me to marry him," she stated, her voice trailing off. The air seemed to leave the truck. David stared out the windshield, his hands tightly gripping the steering wheel, as she continued, "he said he wants me to go with him, but…"

She stopped mid-sentence and left it at that, her gaze returning to survey the passing scenery. Evergreen trees mingled with the edges of the barbed wire fences and secured the borders of the fields.

"But *what*?" David asked, jolting her back to reality. He reached over and put his hand on her shoulder, squeezing it gently. She remembered his words to the boys: Soft touches, she is a girl. "It's me... you can tell me... what is going on?"

"I don't know, really. I mean, on one hand, he said he wanted me to marry him, but on the other hand, I met his family and I didn't make a very good impression. I tried, but I just didn't fit in," she said, her voice shaking at the memory. "When we got back to Springfield, he became more and more distant. He hasn't talked to me in over a week... But I know he is busy, and he said that, with this election, he has some really important issues that he has to take care of. I just think that something has changed... and I am unsure what to do." She felt the tears coming, but took a breath and held them back. Her heart hurt as she thought about being discarded by James.

"You didn't *fit in*?" David asked, then continued without waiting for an answer, "Grace, I have been around people like that. I grew up with people like that. You don't *want* to fit in! They are not worth fitting in with. They chew people up and spit them out. If they can't see your value; you are caring, generous, kind. They aren't *worthy* of being impressed."

Grace sighed and looked across the truck at her friend. She knew he was right, and in her mind believed that, but she didn't yet believe it in her heart. He caught her glance and smiled, trying to reassure her.

"And if he can't see those things that make you really special... well, those traits are the result of your relationship with God. Then it is not you that is unworthy -- it's HIM," he finished.

A Ride Down the Road ©2019

His words hung in the air between them, and she tried to let them sink in so she could believe them. As she was reflecting on what he said, she noticed that the road ahead curved left, then right, between the hills. It wasn't straight and it wasn't flat, but it *was* passable. The sunshine seemed to light the way forward. The trees on either side, with their brown, wispy limbs, lined the road and marked out the way. It brought to mind the picture Grace was so taken by at James' house. The path was not easy, but it was passable, and the light seeping through the trees made it less treacherous. How she longed for that light! But she was starting to see glimpses of it, and she prayed that it would penetrate her heart, even through all her barriers.

Moving on from her reverie, Grace decided to ask David about happenings in the town and what she had missed during her time away. The conversation picked up instantly, and they chatted as if she had never left, just like they always had: as old friends, as confidants. The time passed quickly as they drove through the hills.

"I plan to take over teaching as soon as I return," Grace said, yawning a bit. "I want to give Laura a much-deserved break, and I'm excited to start using what I have learned to help the kids."

"Are you already tired?" he asked, laughing. "That's no way to get started."

"I think that the activities of the week and today, really have made me tired. Lately, I just feel so worn out! But no matter. I will rest this weekend and then start fresh on Monday." She replied with a yawn.

Forward… things were moving forward for her now. She was going home. She was going to her family. Her life would be different, and she would move forward.

A Ride Down the Road ©2019

~ Chapter 15 ~

Lucy drove Grandma down the dirt roads to town for Tucker's game. She chattered on about the journal and letters. She was confused why Grace wouldn't just let go of James.

"It's like he ghosted her before that was a thing," Lucy remarked.

"Ghosted her?" asked Grandma, holding a small handbag in her lap with both hands.

Lucy turned to look at her. The red kerchief in her hair always made Lucy think of the phrase "Put a cherry on top." She smiled to herself, then continued, "Yes, you know, just disappeared like a ghost!" she exclaimed. "He just quit talking to her? What is *that* all about? Just because his family didn't like her, he disappeared."

Lucy zipped down the country roads in the old Buick.
The way it floated up and down and slid around the corners made it feel like a boat on water.

"Slow down, dear. We won't be late. There are 9 whole innings, and these things never seem to go quickly." Grandmas said, bracing herself with the center console. She smelled of the sweet rosewater perfume that she kept in the bathroom. Lucy adored the light scent.

"Sorry, Grandma," said Lucy, slowing the car down a bit and easing up on the corners. "So what's the deal? Was it really like his father said? That he just had his fun with her and moved on? Was he really that shallow? I mean, he wasn't very nice, but to just quit talking to her and not end it well… ugh!"

"His priorities shifted, dear," Grandma said, returning her hands to her handbag. "He was on his way to becoming what he thought he wanted to be... and while, originally, he

A Ride Down the Road ©2019

saw Grace as an asset, he eventually saw her as a distraction or even a hinderance."

"Just like that?!" Lucy said, shaking her head. "Finished? Over?!"

"Well, not exactly, where are you in the story?" Grandma asked.

"Grace just got home and started teaching again." Lucy replied.

"Oh, just keep reading. There it is dear, turn here," Grandma said, pointing to a sign that indicated "baseball fields ahead."

The boat-like Buick rounded the corner and docked in a handicap space close to the field. Tucker was warming up with his teammates and waved when he saw them. Lucy and Grandma made their way to the stands where Kary, Tucker's mom, had saved them a spot on the bleachers.

"Lucy, I have heard so much about you! I thought maybe you would come back by the shop sometime," Kary said, helping Grandma to her seat on a folded tartan blanket. "It's nice to get some time with you today."

Kary was a tall, beautiful black-haired woman with striking features and eyes so dark brown that you couldn't see the pupil. Tanned from the summer sun, she wore a T-shirt that said *I love Junk.* The two chatted until it was time to sing the national anthem. Grandma's friend Val walked on the field, and everyone stood as she sang a gospel rendition of the national anthem, then ended it with a loud "Play Ball!" It was less show-like than her performance at the beauty shop, but Lucy still thought people might break out into a coordinated crowd dance. Val seemed to always be looking for a way to entertain everyone.

Tucker took the mound and opened the game with three straight strikeouts. He coolly walked off the field and into the dugout with nothing more than a simple nod to his mom when she cheered.

"Is he always that calm?" Lucy asked, smiling as she watched her friend get patted on the back by coaches and teammates.

"He is like iced tea on a hot day. He is always *that* calm," his mom said, as she took a sip from her plastic Starbucks cup.

"Ohhh! How close is Starbucks?" Lucy asked, admiring the green goddess-clad cup with hope in her eyes.

"An hour and a half... this is homebrew," Kary replied, looking sadly at the cup. "It's a burden to live this far away from the holy land of Starbucks. But I still make the drive at least once a week to get my coffee fix and do some business."

Lucy laughed at Kary's addiction, acknowledging that she had experienced withdrawal symptoms in the early days of her visit. It could explain the overeating. At least that is what Lucy planned to blame it on, rather than on her weakness around goodies.

"I heard you are reading the journal and letters! Are you loving them?" Kary asked, as a batter made his way to the plate.

"Yes, James Carter was so lovely at the beginning, but then became sooo *not* lovely!" Grace said, wrinkling her nose.

"Pride... ambition... priorities..." Kary replied. "They all change people and make them focus on the wrong things. We all go through it. I certainly did."

"You were like James Carter?" Lucy asked, surprised by the admission.

"Well, lots of people are like him. They may not be as ugly as he was to Grace, but they let other things creep in and change their hearts. Really, he was just a man who let idols in his life -- idols of image and achievement -- cloud his vision of what was good and right," Kary said, clapping for the batter as he hit a single. "Honestly, pride and ambition are two of the main reasons my *marriage* ended."

Lucy was taken aback by her openness and looked surprised. Grandma never took her eyes off the game, but Lucy could tell she was listening.

"Don't worry, everyone here knows everyone else's business, so I talk pretty openly about it," Kary said, as the next batter hit another single. The other team fumbled the ball and the runner advanced to second. "I ran a really successful business and it was my priority... so my husband found someone else who would make *him* her priority. We were *both* wrong."

"Wow, you don't usually hear someone put it *that* way," Lucy said, as Tucker stepped up to the plate, dug his back foot into the dirt, and pulled the bat back.

"Let's Go, Big T!" his mother said, not missing a beat. With that, he swung and popped on to the far outfield on the first pitch. He took off towards first, laying his bat on the ground as he watched the ball. It just missed the back fence. He ran slowly, but his long stride made up for his lack of pace. A double. When he got to the base, he tipped his hat at his mom.

"Well, I am able to say it that way thanks to a lot of therapy sessions with Grandma. Humbleness in recognizing one's part in the demise of a marriage is a hard lesson, but it's necessary for healing." Kary testified, as she nodded back at Tucker and blew him a kiss. He rolled his eyes as the next batter stepped up to the plate.

"We are really close now because I gave it all up. I left the business and started a fresh with a really simple antique store... it barely makes enough to keep the lights on, but I have made up for its lack of traffic with Ebay and an occasional show. Priorities worth having are hard to keep and commit to."

The game went on with lots of conversation and laughter between the women. The Cardinals won, and the team came to the fence and tipped their hats. The crowd chanted, "we're so proud of you! Hay! We're so proud of you! Hay Hay Hay!"

After the game, Tucker came over to greet his adoring fans and pass out sweaty hugs.   He walked Lucy and Grandma to the car.

"I gotta go do a clean-out this afternoon. You want to join me?" he asked Lucy. "I mean, you were so happy to provide free labor last time, so I thought I would invite you again."

"What's a clean-out?" she answered.

"Well, if someone has died or moved away or something, we clean out their house to get inventory for the shop. My mom has a barn out behind our house where she stores her *treasures*… we have more treasures then she could ever sell, but we still do clean-outs," Tucker said.

"That sounds fun," Lucy replied, helping Grandma into the car. They agreed on a time, and he was off.

Lucy drove Grandma home. When they arrived, Grandma went in to make lunch. She told Lucy to go sit on the porch for a while and read. Lucy grabbed the letters and went to the porch, anxious to dive back into the story that had held her attention all summer.

Dearest James

It has been weeks since your last letter.   I am nervous about some things. I am sorry if I made a terrible impression on your family. I know that meant a lot to you. I did try but seemed to not meet the mark. You told me that you love me and want to marry me – is that still so? I really need to talk to you – please call or write soon.

Dear James,

It's been a week since my last letter. I fear that I might be pregnant, and I don't know what to do… I am scared. I am so embarrassed and so overwhelmed. I need you. Please respond.

Grace stood in front of the classroom, exhausted and sick. Her stomach rolled with every scent of leftover lunch and of boys needing a shower. As the room grew hotter throughout the day, she prayed for a breeze to help calm her queasiness.

"Class, let's take out our math books," she started, but felt herself getting light-headed. She tried to steady herself with the desk as the room started to spin.

"Ms. Grace are you ok?" asked one of the older girls, right before Grace collapsed on the floor. When she opened her eyes, Albert's face was two inches from hers wrinkled in worry. Tears were streaming down his cheeks.

"Ms. Grace… Ms. Grace?" he said frantically, his voice desperate. He was holding her hand, almost sitting on top of her. She soon heard footsteps behind him and saw Christopher over the tops of the children's heads.

"Grace!" he said, quickly moving the children aside so he could get to her.

"I am ok. I just got dizzy, that's all. It's probably just the heat," she said, trying to sit up. The room started to move again, and she braced herself by digging her hands into the floor.

"Let me help you home," he said. He barked instructions at the older children to get the younger children home, then asked one of the boys to go get the doctor.

A Ride Down the Road ©2019

"I am ok…" she insisted, as Christopher helped her to her feet. She steadied herself against him, unsure if she could walk without stumbling. "I really don't need a doctor."

Christopher ignored her and helped her down the road to the house. Laura was waiting, the baby in her arms. As soon as she saw them she hurried across the yard to their side.

"What is it?" she asked, grabbing Grace's free hand.

"She passed out at school. I sent one of the boys to get the doctor," Christopher replied. He had one arm around her waist to prop her up, the other hand ready to catch her in case she fell again. They helped Grace to her room. When the doctor arrived, Christopher stepped out, and the doctor examined Grace and then asked her questions.

"Laura, can you give Grace and I a moment?" the doctor asked.

After Laura shut the door behind her, he turned to Grace and asked slowly, "Grace, is there any possibility that you could be pregnant?"

She looked down, not wanting to make eye contact with him. After a long pause, she sighed. "I think I might be…it's… it's been two months or so since..." Her voice trailed off.

"Do you know who the father is?" he asked, trying to make eye contact. She nodded slowly. "Does he know?" he asked.

"Well, I wrote him..." she replied. The shame she felt was so intense that she wasn't sure she could utter any more words. She felt like she had betrayed the trust of the town that cared so much for her.

The doctor sighed, shaking his head, and sat down on the edge of the bed. "Grace, he needs to know, and you two need to be married. Not just because of appearances, but for the *child*. You are young, and, if he is a decent man, he will

A Ride Down the Road ©2019

do the right thing. I don't feel it's my place to tell Christopher and Laura, but they should know too. We all make choices and choices have consequences. Babies are never a bad thing. Just sometimes their timing is not quite what we want. But babies are *always* a blessing, even when the blessing feels like a punishment."

Grace looked up at the doctor, surprised at his kindness. She had expected more of a lecture, or to at least hear some sort of disdain in his voice.

"Grace, I have been a doctor for nearly 50 years. The miracle of conception is always a miracle, even when it does not feel that way. If he says 'no' to marrying you, there are other options for you. There are families that would take a baby whose arrival is not ideally timed."

With that, he patted her hand, got up, and left. She heard him talk in a low voice to her cousins in the hallway. There was a picture of her mom on the table in the room, and it brought tears to her eyes. She picked it up and brought it close to her face, putting her cheek against it, as if she were embracing her mother.

"What should I do, Mom?" she asked the picture, wishing that it would respond with some sort of resounding wisdom. She quickly put it down on the table as Laura walked in the door. "Grace are you ok?" she asked, entering the room. "You don't have to tell me anything but know that I am here for you. No matter what… I am here for you. The doctor said he has done all he can for you and that the sickness will pass in a few weeks."

Grace looked at her blankly. "If she knew, would she still feel this way," she wondered to herself. "If she knew what I have done and the reason I'm sick would she be able to accept me?"

"Laura, I think it's just stress," Grace started, but then stopped short. She knew she couldn't lie to her. She knew

A Ride Down the Road ©2019

Laura would see right through her. She paused, then looked down at her mother's picture.

"Grace, whatever it is, we can handle it together. We are a *family*," Laura replied, her words bathed in kindness.

Grace let the word "family" float in the room like a feather in the wind. She knew that what Laura said was true. She also suspected that this "mistake" might make them change their minds about saying it. But, still, being honest and not keeping secrets from them was the right thing to do, and she knew it. Without waiting another minute in agony, she decided to confess.

"Laura, I'm pregnant."

Grace didn't take her eyes off the picture. She sat there quietly, waiting for the reprimand. For the scolding. The words of disappointment. The room was silent as Grace waited for anger to fill up the space.

But instead of reprimand, scolding, disappointment, or anger, Laura hugged Grace and said, "I love you. We will figure this out. Grace, we will figure this out, we are family, and family takes care of one another. I love you."

Grace was speechless for a second, then burst into tears and sobbed into her cousin's shirt. The embarrassment that this would bring on her cousin -- the tarnishing of their good name. The humiliation of their ward becoming pregnant while in their care. She felt terrible about all of it, and Laura's sweet words were a salve to her soul. Instead of anger, she received love. Acceptance instead of rejection. Support instead of judgement.

We are family, and family takes care of one another.

Grace's greatest fear was being alone and not being able to care for this child. If they threw her out, where would she go? If she was fired from her teaching job, what would she do? Her sin would be visible to everyone in the next few

A Ride Down the Road ©2019

months. She would not be able to hide it like others can hide their sin. Anger, malice, hatred, and lust can be hidden and are often hidden by the "good" and the "faithful." But not this. It would be on display everywhere she went, for all to see and judge.

"Grace, we will help you. We will help take care of you." Laura's forgiveness and acceptance interrupted Grace's thoughts. Her greatest desire was to have a family. She sought it in the arms of a man who promised her all the things she dreamed of, never realizing that she had always had it. That she already had a family who loved her and cared for her.

"I wrote James two weeks ago… but have not heard back." Grace said. "I need to go to him. I need him to know. He said he wanted to marry me. He said he wanted a family."

Laura released Grace and looked into her eyes. "Grace, if he didn't reply… men like him don't live by the same code of honor. They-"

"He said he wanted to marry me…." Grace whispered again, looking at her lap. The room was still until Laura gently laid a hand on her shoulder.

"Then you must go to him," she acknowledged, her eyes filled with apprehension.

"Please don't tell Christopher yet. I will do it later, but I just can't face him yet."

"I won't, but I know he will say the same things that I did. We are never to cast a stone, sweet cousin – we love you and will help you."

The girls talked and derived a plan for Grace to catch a ride with David on his next visit to Springfield. He had to make a delivery twice a month and his next trip was Thursday. When the day of the trip came, Grace joined David in the car. As they drove down the dirt road, she turned and

A Ride Down the Road ©2019

looked at the house with three gables. To her, it would always represent love and acceptance. It would always be her sanctuary.

"So, you are going to visit James?" David asked, as they pulled off on the main highway, headed to Springfield.

"Yes." Grace replied, hoping David wouldn't pry too much. She knew she couldn't lie to him. "I wrote him and let him know I was coming."

"Last we spoke, you hadn't heard much from him. Has that changed?" David asked, staring straight ahead. Grace could tell he was nervous about her visit. Grace sighed and looked out the window. The trees were starting to get their new leaves. The branches from the winter were starting to become full of life again.

"No..." she said slowly, "I haven't heard much from him, but I need to talk to him about something very important."

The cab grew silent again, and Grace busied herself by looking out the window at the trees. The road weaved in and out of the hills as they drove quietly. She wanted to talk to David about what was going on, but she knew it was not the time.

"So how has teaching been going?" David asked, reaching over and giving her a nudge. Immediately, the awkwardness was gone, and they started to chat, just like they always did, about everything and nothing. For a moment, Grace forgot her plight and only heard the voice of her friend. They laughed and talked the whole way to Springfield.

Grace directed David to James' house. He pulled up, and they sat in the parked car. Grace stared at the house, unsure of what to do. In some ways, she wanted James to love her and to be the family he had promised. In other ways, she was afraid of what that life would be like. In regard to his political ambitions and the demands of society life, she knew she would always come in second.

A Ride Down the Road ©2019

"This is it?" he asked, looking up at the majestic craftsman-style house, bordered by a white picket fence. It was like something out of an advertisement. The garden was perfectly manicured, and on the front porch, there were pots of red geraniums leading the way to the massive door. "Yes," she said, smoothing her skirt, her head lowered. She didn't want to leave but knew that she *must*. They sat in silence as she considered staying in the truck and having him turn around and drive her home, but she finally resigned herself to her fate. "I should go," she said, looking over at David. He smiled wearily, as though he wanted to say something but couldn't.

She wondered if he wanted her to stay. Although, it didn't matter. If he knew the truth, then she was sure he would never want to be near her again. She had heard how people spoke of her mother. There were always questions of her respectability because she was a single mother. There were always whispers from the people who knew she was unwed. Even though her husband had left her, something she couldn't have avoided even if she had tried, there were still assumptions.

The stagehands told Grace that no man would want to be with a woman with a child, that no man would want that kind of burden. A religious one talked about the sacrifice a man would have to make to marry a woman like her. Another called her mother "damaged goods". It wasn't until much later that Grace came to realize that none of these statements represented the one true God and his love for his children.

"If you need me… I mean, need a ride, or anything at all…" David said, clearing his throat and handing her a small piece of paper, "This is where I will be today. You can always come home."

The word "home" caught her by surprise. It was a funny thing to say. For a brief moment, she wondered if he knew, but then dismissed the idea. If he did, then he would never leave her there. She smiled thankfully, then turned and got out of the truck. Quickly, she walked through the gate and up to the door. She couldn't bear to look back at David. She knew that if she did, she might not have the courage to continue her journey, to deliver her important message. To talk to James. She rang the doorbell, turning slightly to see if David had left. He sat watching her, then pulled slowly away as the heavy door opened.

~ Chapter 16 ~

Tucker and Lucy drove down a narrow road that curved sharply with the edge of the mountain. It was as if the road was chiseled into the wall.

"Where are you at in the story?" he asked, as he carefully navigated the roads.

"She's pregnant," Lucy replied, looking for glimpses of the lake through the trees. "I was surprised at how the doctor and Grandma reacted... you know, I would think, in those days, that the typical reaction would be to shun her. But maybe that comes later?"

"I think that Grandma has always been unique in how she cares for and loves people. She doesn't see their sin. She has told me for years that we need to see people the way God sees them," Tucker said, "That He created them as His children and that they're worthy of His love. Sin is something everyone has in common. We *all* sin so deciding that some sins are worse than others is a sin in its own right. I like her perspective: *Love* people. It's pretty simple" Tucker slowed the truck to take a corner then turned onto a small side road. Soon, they pulled up in front of a long, narrow, 1950s rambler ranch house overlooking the edge of the cliff.

"This is it," he said, parking the truck and waving a hand towards the house. It looked like it had been frozen in time. In the front yard there were two deer made of stone, and a bird bath standing between them.

"You know, it's where we all screw things up with faith," Tucker said, leaning forward onto the steering wheel. "We try to make someone else's sin seem worse than our own. But *all* sin separates us from God, and all people need a savior. So why should I ever treat someone differently because their sin seems greater than mine. I mean, didn't Jesus die for all of it? Wouldn't have even the 'smallest' sin still have sent Him to the cross?"

A Ride Down the Road ©2019

"Wow, you are *amazing*," Lucy replied, looking over at her friend, her eyes wide. "How do you come up with this stuff?! I mean, it's so… *wise*… like, who ARE you?" she laughed.

Tucker shook his head. "They're not my words. Have you ever read Christopher's sermons?" he grinned, looking back at her. "Come on, let's go knock this out."

"So, the person didn't die here, right?" Lucy asked nervously, slowly climbing out of the truck. "I mean, like... they died somewhere else, right?"

Tucker laughed. "Dunno. Honestly, I don't ask. The money is good, and I need it for college. Plus, Mom likes the finds. That's why we pull the big trailer. She and Ethan will be here shortly."

When they got to the front of the house, Tucker unlocked the door and opened it carefully. The house reeked of mothballs and dust. He took a long, deep breath.

"Nothing like the smell of a good, vintage house," he chucked, coughing a bit. "You know, an *antique* is something that's been around for at least 100 years. If it's just *old*, then it's called *vintage*."

Lucy rolled her eyes as they walked into the small entryway. Lucy cringed as she eyed the room: the carpet, couch, chairs, and wall-paper were all white. The couch and chair had plastic covers on them, and a well-worn plastic walkway stretched across the carpet. The carpet, white thought it was, was pristine, as if no one had ever stepped foot off of the plastic path. A white china cabinet sat against the far wall, filled with blue and white dishes, figurines, and other knick-knacks. Lucy guessed they must all be expensive.

"Did you put down all this plastic?" she asked, staring into the cabinet. Tucker flopped down on the couch, creating a cloud of dust that rose to the ceiling and made Lucy cough.

"Nope, and not on the couch either. This was the way they kept the house when they lived here. The estate attorney let us know that they didn't have children or anything, just a house full of stuff. The whole house is to be emptied. There's no next of kin. He said to just clean it out and that he'd put it up for sale."

He got up and motioned for her to follow him, walking through the dining room and then into the kitchen. It was straight out of the 1970s, with avocado green appliances. appliances were avocado green. The once-bright-orange, plaid backsplash stood out against the dark wood stain of the cabinets. It was a *sight*.

"Well, this is a total gut job," Tucker laughed, as he tapped the yellow counters. They both giggled. They walked past the octagon-shaped table and accompanying large round pendant chandelier. On one side of the kitchen, you could look into the family room and see the brown and orange shag carpet that looked like it needed to be raked, not vacuumed. On the other side of the kitchen was a wall of windows that looked out over a large deck. They both walked to the window and marveled at the view.

The bridge from Kimberling City (which used to be the town of Radical) could be seen in the East. The hills were speckled with houses that overlooked the snake-like lake. They paused for some time, staring at the view. Then Lucy broke the silence.

"That's incredible," she sighed, stepping back and tripping over the magazine rack that leaned up against a recliner. She caught herself on the built-in bookshelf, packed full of what looked like a century's worth of National Geographic Magazines.

Tucker snapped out of his trance. "So, we go through and make three piles: trash, donate, and keep." Tucker explained, stepping away from the window and looking around the room. He ran his hands across the wood-paneled walls and stopped at a painting. "For example, this

A Ride Down the Road ©2019

painting of the lake, my mom will totally want to keep that. While most of us just see a homemade painting, Kary sees a masterpiece." He picked up a notepad with scribbled items. "However, this notepad is definitely trash. Easy enough?" he asked, walking towards the door. "I'll be right back; I need to grab the trash bags. You okay to stay here?" he joked, walking out the door.

"I am," she replied, leaning in to get a better look at the National Geographic magazines. She wondered if Kary would keep all of them. Their yellow spines were in good condition.

"He died in *that* chair," Tucker called, letting the screen door slam behind him. Lucy glanced over at the chair and cringed, then rolled her eyes. She turned back to the magazines, picking one up to flip through pictures of the jungles of Africa, then put it back and opened the lower cabinet doors.

There were jars of coins, dozens of them, and labeled with what looked like a waitress pad noting the day and the total amount. It was as if a waitress had thrown her tips in there, storing them up for a rainy day. Lucy picked one up and shook the jar, which uncovered a mix of coins, matchbooks, and even a pencil or two.

Tucker walked back in and saw her find. "Jackpot!" he laughed. He stopped short when he realized the entire cabinet was filled with jars. "Wow, we may need to ask my mom what to do!"

"Ask me what?" Kary's voice came from behind them as she appeared, her arms full of plastic bins.

"Hi, Mom!" Tucker said with a smile, leaning down to kiss her on the cheek. "What do we do with all this? Do we need to call the estate attorney?"

"Nope. I bought the house with all contents," she replied. "Maybe we just located the down payment!"

A Ride Down the Road ©2019

"What? You bought the house? I thought this was a clean out!"

"Well, it was a good price, and I think we could update it and rent it out in the summers."

"Mom…" Tucker said, sighing and shaking his head.

"I don't have room at the shop for all the things, so I thought, 'Hey, why not just buy a furnished house that you could update? Then I could and I could rent it out!'"

"Mom's brilliant mind at work!" laughed Tucker, shrugging.

They spent the day going through the whole house and taking out bags of trash. The bags were mostly full of old, faded Cool Whip containers that had been used for years to store leftovers. In the bedrooms, they found a closet full of clothes with the tags on them, along with stacks of pictures of a woman and her husband. Grace took on the project of emptying the closet. Tucker, having found a radio, was blasting country music from the other room, singing along at the top of his lungs. As she pulled out vintage suits, hats, and shoes, she thought about the journal entry she read earlier that day.

David drove me to Springfield, and I thought I knew what to expect, but it turns out I had no idea what was waiting for me there...

LuElla opened the door, shocked to see Grace.

"Hello, LuElla." Grace said, relieved to have her as a buffer before she had to see James.

"Ms. Grace!" she said quickly, looking over her shoulder. Then she leaned in towards Grace and said in a hushed tone, "What are you doing here?"

"I am here to see James," Grace said, confused as to why LuElla seemed so nervous. "Is he home?"

LuElla hesitated, then started to close the door. "You gonna have to come back again some other time. He can't see you right now."

Grace put her hand on the door, stopping it from closing. She studied LuElla's face. "But I need to see him," she insisted, frantically trying to see past her into the house. "It's important – can you please get him for me?"

Grace could smell dinner cooking and heard the radio playing in the parlor. She thought about pushing her way in and bursting in on whatever meeting James was having in the house.

"He is busy. Really, Ms. Grace, please come back later. I am sorry." LuElla reiterated and attempted again to push the door closed. "You don't understand, Ms. Grace..."

"Who is it, LuElla?" Grace winced as she heard a familiar voice come up behind LuElla and saw James appear behind her. Realizing it was Grace, he quickly stepped in front of LuElla and onto the porch, then glared at LuElla as he closed the door behind him.

"What are you doing here?" he groused, sealing the door of his house.

"I came to see you," she said, trying to hide her fear behind a smile. Taking his hand, she continued, "I need to talk to you about my letter." He quickly pulled his hand away and stepped back, straightening his tie.

"Grace, I... uh …I can't talk to you today. Another time, perhaps. You should go," James grunted, walking backwards towards the house and then tripping over the small pot of geraniums. He reached for the bronze colored doorknob, uncomfortably trying to escape the conversation.

"Another time?" she asked, wringing her hands. "Did you read my letter?" her voice quaked. "What's wrong? Please don't go... I need your help."

A Ride Down the Road ©2019

"If you must know... well, I can't see you anymore," he said fidgeting with his suit. His words punched her in the gut, and she took a step back.

"You can't see me anymore? But my *letter….*"

"You see, I realize now that, to run for office, I need someone who can thrive in that world. Someone who can support me fully," he reasoned. He continued to talk, but his explanations of why they could no longer see each other swirled around Grace like the tornadoes she had read about in the newspapers, with pieces of debris knocking her one way and then the other. "You need to move on. You will find someone else," he assured her.

"Move on?" she asked, her head was spinning from the barrage of heartless words. Her mind raced as she reasoned with herself that he must not have received her letters. He would never just dismiss her this way if he knew.

"Did you get my letter? Do you *know…*?!" she started.

"I did," he responded matter-of-factly. Horrified, she began to realize that his intentions had not been true. She felt the color fall from her face as she steadied herself on the rail. James paused, looking away from her. She wondered what he was thinking, wondered if maybe he was reconsidering. However, his response seemed crafted, as if he were answering a reporter and not the woman he had professed to love. Not for the woman he had asked to marry him. "I am sorry about your situation," he ended his statement. It was like the final blow in a constant torrent of cruelty, but it jolted Grace back into the present.

"*Situation*?!" she exclaimed, wanting to slap him back into reality. Just then, the door opened, and James' mother appeared with the beautiful blonde from the dinner at the governor's mansion

"James is something wrong?" his mother asked him, looking at Grace in surprise.

James stammered out an answer. It was full of lies about how Grace was in town and stopped by to say hello. Grace stared blankly at his mother, then at the blonde behind her. She looked perfect in her blue suit with matching bag and shoes, her hair pinned back like it was the last time she saw her. She was all made up like the models in the magazines. Grace could only imagine what *she* looked like in comparison. She was sick to her stomach, tired from the ride, and sure her hand-me down dress was wrinkled.

"I thought you took care of that," James' mother said, pointing at Grace.

"*That.*" The word rattled in Grace's head, bouncing off the walls of her skull as it sank into her mind. "That," as if she was just an object that needed to be dealt with, not a person. She took a deep breath and looked at James, wishing he would say something. But just like before, he said nothing. He just looked at the ground. Grace shook her head in disbelief, then walked down the steps to the street. She wasn't sure where to go or what to do, she just wanted to be away. She needed to be far away from *him*. She stumbled aimlessly down the street, then heard footsteps behind her.

"Grace, stop!" James said, running up behind her and grabbing her arm. She quickly pulled her arm away. Every ounce of anger and rage boiled up in her body as she spun around to face him.

She began to spew her words at him, "Take care of *THAT* – I am a *that?!* I am not even a *person* to her! Does she know? Does she know that I am carrying her *grandchild*!"

"Shh...Shh..." James said, putting his finger to his lips, "Please... keep your voice down. Let's not make a scene."

"A scene?! We are *way* past a scene! We are way past *anything* civilized or discrete!" she exploded, waving her arms wildly in the air, "You said you loved me! You said you wanted to marry me and have a family! Well, here I am!

A Ride Down the Road ©2019

Here I am ready to be that family with you and carrying your *child*!"

"Grace! *Please* keep your voice down," he begged, grabbing her arm tightly and squeezing it. He jerked her close to him pulling her onto the sidewalk as he tried to reason, "I can't. You know I can't do this right now." His voice broke as he continued, "I am sorry! I really am sorry... but I *can't* right now. It's not good timing for me."

"Right now, is all I have," she retorted. Her voice cracked as she tried to make him understand. "This baby won't wait for your convenience." She searched his face for some shift in decision. "This is our *child,* and *now* is the time for you to remember what you said to me. What you *promised* me," she implored him. Grace started choking back tears and feared she would fall to pieces.

For a moment, she thought he might change his mind. He looked at her the way he looked at her the first time the met.
   Desperately, she reached for his hand again, shaking so hard that she thought she might collapse.

Out of nowhere, James' mother walked up behind him and slid her hand over his shoulder. "James, it's time to go," she hissed.

He closed his eyes. Grace wondered if he considered walking away from it all and staying with her. She wished he would, but just to hide their sin. It wasn't about love anymore. She knew she didn't love him. Grace knew she could never respect someone who lied to his family and was too weak to stand up for others he claimed to love. Rather, she just he wished he would help her not be labeled, not be alone in bearing the burden of the scarlet letter. *He* could walk away unscathed. *He* could ignore her, and the world would never know, because men don't have the public humiliation of a pregnancy outside of the "right" timeline. The religious community shuns the mother as a failure, and the general public labels her as irresponsible. James could make all of those perceptions go away. He could make it all

A Ride Down the Road ©2019

be just a hushed conversation instead of a public humiliation.

When James opened his eyes, she knew it was over. His stare was vacant and his voice icy. "I am sorry, Grace, there is nothing I can do to help you with your situation. You should go. Please don't bother me anymore," he stated coldly.

Grace watched as he turned and walked away. His mother slipped her hand into the crook of his arm as she looked over her shoulder, glaring at Grace. The words came back to her, the words James had thrown at her so heartlessly. Her "situation" it cut her to the core as she realized that her whole life had felt like one situation after another.

"I told you that girls like her are just looking for a ticket out of their situation. They are always in trouble, looking for money or support or something," she said loud enough for Grace to hear.

Girls like her... orphaned and poor... now pregnant with no husband... girls like *her*. Something in her heart shifted as she started to believe she had no worth. Laura's words of love were fighting their way through the darkness of the hate that clouded her heart. She felt a battle going on for her soul. The evil of world fighting against hope and value that Laura and Christopher worked so hard to instill in her. "But God demonstrates his love for us in this, while we were still sinners - Christ died for us." *Worthy*... the word kept coming up again and again. *Worthless...* the word kept attacking. *Created...* but why would God create someone like her? Someone who fails over and over again? Why would he create someone destined to disappoint Him? "How great is the love the Father has lavished on us - that we should be called the children of God, and that is what we are...." Created as His child. Her heart shattered into so many pieces that day that she was unsure if anyone, including God, could piece it back together.

A Ride Down the Road ©2019

Grace turned and started to walk towards town. She wasn't sure where to go or what to do, so she walked to a park. Children played and women walked together talking about the day. They had no idea that her world was falling apart.

"What do I do, Lord? What do I do? If You will only forgive me for all of this… I am not sure how You can forgive me, but please. Help me. Help me know what to do," she prayed fervently.

She found a bench and sat until the day turned to dusk. The air was chilly. She shoved her hands in her pockets and found the note from David. It was a name and an address. For a moment, she considered staying on the bench and never going back to Laura and Christopher. Maybe that would save them the embarrassment. But she heard Laura's words over and over "We are *family,* you can always come home."

Slowly, she got up and walked to the address. As she neared, she saw David standing next to his truck, talking to a man. The house was a parsonage behind a long rectangular brick church. He spotted her and smiled.

"Grace, I didn't expect to see you!" he said, happily walking over to her. "We were just going in for dinner."

As she watched him approach, everything started to hit her at once. Suddenly, Grace couldn't contain the tears, and she started to cry.

"Oh, Grace, I am so sorry. Things must not have gone well." He quickly hugged her as they stood in the street. "It's ok. He didn't deserve you... he never deserved you."

David's words comforted her, like bandages for her heart. She rested her head against his chest, took a deep breath, and collected herself.

"I want to go home," she whispered, listening to his heartbeat.

A Ride Down the Road ©2019

"Yes, I will take you home," he replied, squeezing her tightly.

A Ride Down the Road ©2019

~ Chapter 17 ~

Tucker and Lucy drove up to the dirt road to Grandma's house joking and laughing about the day's adventure. The house had more treasures hidden away than anticipated, and Kary had danced with glee every time one was found. Lucy started to wonder if she saw the antique shop as her own personal museum instead of an area of commerce.

Lucy loved it here. Something about the air was different than home. Maybe it was cleaner, or maybe the cow patties elicited the sweet smell of a slower pace. She loved that she knew everyone at church after just a few visits and that everyone treated each other like family. Even the occasional drama resolved itself because someone would remind another of their purpose as a church. She loved that things were simple and unrushed. It was peaceful and perfect. As they neared the house, she saw a familiar car in the driveway.

"Wonder who that is?" he asked, pulling past the car on the grass and parking at the barn. Lucy took a deep breath as she realized her world was going to change soon. She didn't want to answer at first. Maybe if she didn't say anything, it would mean it didn't have to be the end of her summer. Finally, she took a deep breath.

"It's my mother," Lucy replied.

"Are you leaving soon?" he asked, gripping the steering wheel and rubbing the sides of it.

"I don't know... I didn't think so," she said, slumping down in her seat. She wished that they had not left the stinky house with the great view. They sat silently in the car outside the house.

"I've had fun spending time with you. I know this summer has been hard, but it will get better. I know it will get better," he said, nudging her arm. Lucy thought she might cry. Leaving was the last thing she wanted to do. Walking back

A Ride Down the Road ©2019

into the chaotic mess of her parents lives right now was overwhelming. Tucker nudged her again. "Hey, chin up! We can keep in touch. We have phones even out here in the sticks. We can write, too, seeing as you seem to enjoy all the letters you've been reading."

Lucy looked over at her friend and smiled. His wavy brown hair was messy and sticking out from under the edges of his red cap. She wished she could take a picture and save this moment.

He grinned at her. "You should go see your mom," he said, nodding towards the house.

"Do you want to come in?" she asked, hopeful she would not have to go in alone. He looked past her to the house and shook his head. "Nah, I think you need some time with her," he replied, "It will be ok. You've got this."

Lucy leaned over and hugged him. "Thanks for everything," she said, quickly getting out of the car and walking to the house. She looked back several times. She was unsure of what the future held, and she didn't really want to leave the present. She stopped at the door and waved before walking into the kitchen.

Her mom and Grandma sat at the table talking and drinking coffee from the green jadite mugs that Lucy cleaned earlier that day. She smiled as she remembered how excited Kary had gotten over the Fire King dishes she found at the house. A milk glass cake plate with a ruffled edge full of cookies sat between them inviting her to join. Lucy's mom jumped up and hugged her.

"Oh, my sweet girl, I've missed you!" she said. She took Lucy's face in her hands and kissed her forehead.

"I missed you too. What are you doing here mom?" Lucy asked, studying her face. She seemed older and worn out, as if she had not been sleeping.

"Well, I came to get you and bring you home," she replied, stepping back to the table and sitting down. She motioned for Lucy to join them. Lucy grabbed a cookie and sat down at the table.

"I moved all of your things to your new room, and...," her mom started.

"Wait," Lucy interjected, "Moved my things? What happened to the house?" She realized that more had changed than just her parents' marriage.

"Well… we had to sell the house. We *had* to," her mom explained.

"You sold the house! What do you mean you sold the house?" Lucy interrupted, frustrated by the idea of her home being gone.

"We had to sell the house to divide the asset," her mom said, her tone business like.

"The 'asset'?" Lucy repeated, staring at the wood grain in the table, her anxiety level rising. Her chest felt tight. When did her home become an *asset* to be divided? "My home…"

Lucy wanted to run to the grove of trees, the one where she liked to sit and read, anything to get out of that room and that conversation. Her mom kept talking, kept calling her "Luce", and kept trying to explain how great it was going to be at the new place.

"I told you that I want to stay here," Lucy replied, looking helplessly at her Grandma. "I want to stay and take care of Grandma this year. I can finish up school here, and I can…"

"Lucy, you know that you can't do that," her mom interjected, "Transferring your senior year? That's an awful idea. All of your hard work would be wasted, and, besides, your friends are at home."

A Ride Down the Road ©2019

"Mom, I'm not going with you. I am staying here," Lucy insisted, taking her hand and giving it a squeeze. "I love you, but you've made your choices, and I am old enough to make this decision." The room was quiet as Lucy's mom looked at her daughter, dumbfounded.

"I am going to bed," Lucy said, as she got up and walked towards her room. She quickly went inside and closed the door behind her, then leaned against it, sighing. She didn't want this summer to end. It was awful and wonderful all at the same time. She walked to the window and gazed up at the stars sprinkled across the night sky, almost as if God had poured them out of a saltshaker. The face of the man in the moon glowed a deep shade of yellow, clear and inviting, as if he wanted her to sit there at the window and converse with him. She wondered why she had never noticed the moon and the stars at home

She could hear her mom and Grandma talking in the hallway, saying something about getting rest and how things would be easier in the morning. Lucy climbed into bed and pulled out the journal.

Standing in the middle of that street, watching James and his mother walk away broke my heart into a million pieces. I was left there like a bag of trash is left on the corner to be picked up -- discarded like a worthless piece of garbage. I walked to a park and saw children playing, and my heart ached, wondering if my child will be happy like that, or outcast... because of me. I was lucky that David had not left and could take me back to Christopher and Laura's house...

Grace was thankful that the pastor and his wife graciously let her stay at their home that night. Grace was quiet through dinner as she observed how the pastor and his wife spoke to one another and cared for their family. The pastor's words were always kind and gracious to his wife, and she always responded in a way that exuded respect and admiration of his work. Their children were polite, although still a little ornery. One of the boys tried to scoop his peas onto his brothers' plate when he wasn't looking, which caused a bit of

A Ride Down the Road ©2019

a commotion. It was everything Grace wanted for her life. A family, even with its imperfections, was her dream.

After dinner Grace, slept in the room with the younger girls. She looked out the window at the night sky. Stars were everywhere, and the moon was a beautiful shade of gold. She stared at its smiling face as it bathed the room with warm light. Maybe things would be clearer to her in the morning. She could hear Laura's words as she dozed off, "God's Mercies are new each day. Great is his faithfulness."

Early the next morning, David and Grace got into the truck to head home. The town went by as they drove in the early hours. A large round Texaco light shined brightly at the station where they stopped for gas. As the man filled the tank for them, David stepped out and chatted with him. Grace exhaled, trying to rid herself of memories from the day before, thinking maybe she could expel the burdens with her breath. But they remained. Where was "the peace that passes understanding"? Where was the hope?

"Lord, I need You as my refuge," she thought as she ran her hands over her swelling abdomen. *"I need Your guidance and pardon. Please care for me and this baby. I beg You for help."*

"Well, let's go home," David said, climbing into the truck and smiling at Grace. She weakly smiled back, then returned her gaze to the town rolling by outside the window. Men in business suits walked quickly down the street, and stores began to open their doors for business. People seemed busy and determined to get where they were going, with little concern for the world around them. It was just another morning for them, but for Grace it was a morning filled with questions, hurt, and confusion.

As they turned onto the highway to get back home, David began to uncomfortably run his hands over the steering wheel. They drove for miles with no words, just the sound of the truck on the road, until David broke the silence.

A Ride Down the Road ©2019

"Do you want to talk about it?" David asked. Grace took a deep breath and leaned her head against the window. She wasn't sure she could handle talking about it or reliving it at all.

"He decided to move on," she finally said, not lifting her head from the window. "Apparently, I am not right for him and his future. He found someone new." She didn't have any emotion left in her. No tears. The pain had been so intense yesterday that she couldn't muster the strength to be emotional, at least not about James.

"Well, good riddance!" David grunted, "He was never good enough for you. I mean that. We all thought the same thing. He was not even *close* to worthy." Grace caught David's eye as she glanced up from her slouched position in the car.

"I mean that. You are --" he started but hesitated as he seemed to be considering what to do next. Suddenly, he turned onto a dirt road.

"Where are we going?" Grace asked, knowing that this was not the normal way home. David drove the truck into the grass of an open field and parked under a large tree. The field was green and the tree was budding with new life.

"Grace, I need to tell you something," David said, taking a deep breath. Grace looked over at him, but he kept staring straight forward as he continued. "I need you to know... I need you to know that I have feelings for you… and... Grace, it's more than just *feelings…*"

Her heart sank into her stomach. "Not now... why *now*?" she thought, anxiously clasping her hands.

"I have for a long time. You are smart, caring, kind, and genuine. You are everything I have ever wanted in my life. I look forward to every moment we spend together. That's why I always volunteered to drive you to college. I can't wait each week for Sundays when I get to see you at church and spend the afternoon with you. I love you," he said, reaching

A Ride Down the Road ©2019

over and touching her arm. She didn't respond, but her hands kept going to the side of her face to wipe away tears. "I know that a divorced man is not ideal. I am a flawed man, but I would do anything to care for you and have you as my wife."

The word "love" seemed to float across the space and into her lap. "If he only knew... if he only knew what I have done. He could not love me. He would not want anything to do with me," she thought, as she cried quietly. She was staring out the window but could hear him running his hands nervously along the sides of the steering wheel.

"Grace," he said, reaching over and again touching her arm, "I know this is probably too soon, but you need to know."

She turned and looked at him, her face stained with tears.

"I am sorry – I shouldn't have upset you," he said, eyes wide as he nervously gripped the steering wheel with one hand.

"It's not you." she said, starting to sob uncontrollably. "It's not you." She cried so hard her body started to shake. He quickly scooted across the cab and held her. Time stood still as her brokenness poured out.

"It wasn't fair of me to say anything. I am so sorry," he said pressing his face against her hair. How she longed to live in this moment, being held by this man.

"David…" she whispered, her face still buried in his shirt, "I am pregnant." She braced herself for him to recoil and look at her with disgust, but he only squeezed tighter.

"Oh, Grace," David said with a warm, steady tone. He squeezed her tighter and kissed the top of her head.

"I know it was wrong. I knew then and I know now. He said he loved me, and, honestly, I felt like I loved him, too. I didn't want him to question it. I knew it was wrong and I went ahead with it. I am such a fool," Grace sobbed.

A Ride Down the Road ©2019

"We will take care of you – Laura, Christopher, and I – you are our family," David replied softly, trying to reassure her.

"Christopher doesn't know," she said, and David sat back and smiled.

"That makes more sense. If he knew, he would have ridden with me to go take care of him," he chuckled, running his hand across the dash of the truck. They stared out the front window. Outside the truck, the world continued. The clouds went by and birds flew from branch to branch on a nearby tree, fully unaware of Grace's crisis. Grace was reminded of Laura's scripture. "Look at the birds of the air… are you not more valuable than them to your heavenly Father. Why do you worry?"

David reached up to her face and gently brushed away the hair. She looked over at him and could tell he was searching for words. Instead, he reached over and pulled her close to him again.

"He didn't care," she said, taking a deep breath. His flannel shirt smelled of firewood and fields. "He told me he loved me and told me he wanted to be a family. Now, he will be a father, and he doesn't care. He said he was sorry about my 'situation'. He called it a *situation*. But it's a *child*."

"If he were a father, or a *real* man, he would have never done anything that could put you in this position in the first place. And, even had it happened like it did, he would have let nothing stop him from getting to you once he got that letter. He would have dropped everything and came!" David said, tension rising in his voice. He pulled back from her and took her hands gently in his. Grace had never seen him angry, nor really ever heard him raise his voice. He was always calm and collected. "If he had any brain at *all*, then he would have never let you go." David's hands were warm and safe. He ran his thumbs lightly across the top of hers.

"But he did," Grace lamented. "Now, I am alone to care for this child. Everyone will know and be so disappointed." How she wished she could turn back time and change the past.

"Family takes care of one another. Family does not forsake one another just because something doesn't line up perfectly. You know that Laura and Christopher would never let you be alone and deal with this on your own," he reminded her.

They stared at each other. Grace wanted nothing more than to be held again in his arms, but was afraid that, as he processed what was going on, he would change his mind about loving her. She remembered back to when she was young and would overhear the stagehands and people in New York talking about her and her mother. One woman had even dared to tell her, "Regardless of one's beauty, no man wants to be responsible for another man's child. Your mother will always be alone"

She looked at her hands resting on her lap. "Why did I fail you, Lord? Why didn't I wait for what was good? Why didn't I wait for your perfect timing?" she agonized.

The cab was silent again. David was silent, still staring out the front window. Grace wondered if he was analyzing the way to move forward. There was no road, no definition of where to go, just a field. It would be easier to back up and turn around than forge a new path to the highway, but he kept looking forward.

"Would you marry me?" he asked, after a long moment, as if he had discovered the way. "I can't offer much, but I can offer you family and a commitment to always love and care for you. I wouldn't expect anything from you. I know this is sudden. I'd just be a partner and a friend. I know this may not be what you had in mind, but I *would* be a good husband and a good father."

Grace was stunned. Her mind raced as she tried to process what he was saying. Unlike James, who pursued her with talk of marriage for his *own* benefit, David would benefit nothing from marrying her. He wasn't bargaining or trying to gain something from her by doing this.

"What?" she asked in disbelief, trying to determine if this was real.

He grabbed her hand and squeezed it lightly as he continued, "Marry me!"

Her heart raced so fast in her chest she thought it might explode. She was not sure what to do. David was her friend. In some ways, he was as close to her as Laura was. She did care for him. She knew that he would be good to her but questioned if this was the right thing to do, if it would really be fair to him.

"David, I am pregnant. You don't want me," she said, searching his face. She rubbed her emerging bump as she continued, "You don't want this. You don't want the ridicule. People will still know."

He smiled, trying to reassure her. "I want *you* and whatever you bring with you. I will take care of you and the baby. I know this must seem crazy to you. I know it seems impulsive, but I have been thinking about marrying you for a long time. I just didn't say anything, but I should have. I should have told you."

"I...," she stuttered, completely unsure of what to do. She looked back out the front window into the open field. There was no way forward in her mind. No way to navigate the unknown. "I can't do that to you. This is too much of a burden for me to put on you. You are good and decent. And the boys --I love them so much. What if they are ridiculed because of me?"

The smile left David's face as he sat back in his seat. "You aren't *doing* anything to me. I am a grown man and I know what I am doing. I am asking you to marry me... and the boys love you. Grace, I *love* you. I know you've heard that

A Ride Down the Road ©2019

before from someone who *didn't* love you, someone who was after their own selfish interests. But *this* is not *that... this* is real. But I understand if you don't love me and don't want to be married to me. I have always just wanted you to be happy."

"I care for you deeply," she replied, staring blankly at the field in front of them, too overwhelmed to make eye contact, "but I can't do that to you." As soon as the words left her mouth, she immediately regretted it. What was she thinking? This was a good opportunity for her. This was an answer to her problem. This would solve her plight. But that was the problem, it was all about her. She feared that it was just a good opportunity, an answer to a problem, and not the best for David. He deserved the best, and she feared that this would not be the best for him. There was silence in the car for what felt like an eternity. Grace was sure that David took her words as rejection, not understanding her desire to protect him from her humiliation.

David shifted the car into drive. "I'll take you home."

They drove in silence to the house with three gables. David slowly drove up the driveway and parked next to the house. The boys barreled out the front door as Grace and David climbed out of the truck. Ben ran to his dad, and Albert ran to Grace. In typical Albert-style, he nearly knocked her over with his hug. Laura emerged from the house, wiping her hands on a kitchen towel that was tucked in her waistline. When she spotted Grace, she hurried to embrace her cousin.

"Things didn't go as planned?" she asked with a look of concern. Grace shook her head and held back tears. "It will be ok... it really will," Laura consoled her, taking her hand and walking her inside. "David, lunch is on the table. Come on in and help yourself," Laura said, looking over her shoulder. David nodded, taking Ben by the hand, and walked in behind them.

"Dad, I helped with lunch. I cut up the potatoes," Ben said proudly, as he rambled on about his adventures with Christopher.

Lunch was filled with long silences and awkward exchanges. Christopher tried to elicit conversation, asking about his friends in Springfield and how the deliveries went. It was obvious there was something hanging in the air when David answered. Christopher and Laura kept looking at one another throughout the meal, and Grace could tell that they were trying to discern what had happened. As the meal ended, Christopher asked David to join him on the back porch. The boys went out to play, and the cousins started to clear the table. Grace watched the men walk to the tree line and disappear down the path. She was so distracted that she almost dropped a dish.

"Grace," Laura said, grabbing the dish before it crashed to the counter. "*What* is going on?"

"Does Christopher know?" Grace asked Laura, as she tried to focus on the dishes and carefully cleaned the remaining plates.

"Yes," Laura replied, "I'm sorry, but I had to tell him after you left. He was very upset that I let you go at all."

"I told David," Grace said, picking up the wet plates and gently wiping them with the feed sack cloth that she had embroidered for Laura for her birthday. It had bright flowers tied with a blue ribbon.

"What did he say?" Laura asked, acting as an assembly line as she picked up the dried plates and put them away.

"He asked me to marry him," Grace said, setting the plate down. She turned and looked at her friend hopelessly. "And I said no..."

A Ride Down the Road ©2019

Laura was shocked. Her brow furled as she slowly responded, "David is never impulsive, Grace. He never does anything that isn't well thought out. I am surprised..."

"But he didn't at first. He told me that James didn't deserve me and that he had fallen in love with me... it was only after I told him about the baby that he asked. I know that he is trying to help me, but I can't do that to him, Laura. I can't burden him with this."

Laura sat down at the small, round, maple table and ran her hand along its smooth edge. She motioned for her friend to join her. "Sweet girl, David is smart and kind and thoughtful. If he asked, then he meant it. He understands the burden. He has lived in a world of judgement and burden for a long time. He has two boys all on his own. If he told you he loves you, then he does, and he does not care what others may think or say. The question isn't about him, it's about *you*. Do you love him? Right now, it might not be a passionate love, you are too hurt for that. But think about what he means to you," Laura implored.

They heard the men coming back towards the house. Grace glanced out the window and saw that Christopher had put his arm around David's shoulder, like a big brother would do to offer comfort. As they approached the house, David told the boys to go get in the truck. They obliged and raced to the back, laughing and playing tag the whole way.

"Grace, can I talk to you?" David inquired, as he and Christopher walked into the kitchen. She nodded, following him out the door and down the front path. He stopped, staring at the truck and smiling weakly as the boys waved from inside the cab.

"I want you to know that it's ok that you didn't say yes today. I am not sure what I was thinking about putting that out there like that. You have been through so much," he said, still looking at the truck. Grace felt her heart sink into her stomach.

A Ride Down the Road ©2019

"David, I am sorry," she started, looking up at him, her voice shaking, but he held his hand up nervously as he interrupted.

"No, no, *I* am sorry," he interrupted looking back at her, "the timing was wrong, and I should not have put all of that on you." Grace wanted to throw her arms around him and tell him yes, but she didn't.

"I need you to know something. I need you to know that my feelings have not changed, nor will they. Whenever you are ready, if you are ever ready," he began, but the boys started calling him from the truck. He quickly looked over his shoulder and motioned for them to quiet down, then stated, "I am here."

With that, he turned, shoved his hands in his pockets, and rushed to his vehicle.

Grace watched and waved as they drove away. "What kind of love was this?" she marveled.

~ Chapter 18 ~

The noisy rooster stood outside Lucy's window and crowed loudly. She covered her head with a pillow as he repeatedly declared morning's arrival.

"You, I won't miss," she said, rolling over in her bed. The ceiling fan went round and round as it moved the warm air through the room. It was just enough to make the papers on the desk flap up and down.

The idea of going back with her mom and leaving this place of peace was dreadful. Questions rolled through her head on how life would change: alternating between two houses and making each one her residence, watching her parents move on, and all of the other miserable things her friends with divorced parents described. She didn't believe either place would ever be "home", and she knew her family would never again be whole. Lucy exhaled loudly. She did not want to get out of the bed even though the smell of fresh biscuits seeped under the door and beckoned her to come to the kitchen. She did not want this summer just to become some set of wonderful memories that ended up in a picture frame.

There was a knock at the door, and Lucy's mother let herself into the room.

"Luce… are you up?" she asked, as she walked over to the bed and sat on the edge of it. Her mom gently rubbed Lucy's feet.

"Yes," Lucy mumbled, still staring at the ceiling fan.

"There are biscuits," her mother replied, "and you know there's nothing better than Grandma's biscuits and gravy!"

"I know…" Lucy sighed.

"I know all of this doesn't make sense and that it's hard," her mother reasoned, "but it had to happen."

A Ride Down the Road ©2019

"Why?" Lucy inquired, rubbing the sleep from her face. "Why did it have to happen?" She sat up in bed and hugged her knees to her chest, staring at her mother. "Did someone have an affair? Is that what happened?" Lucy inquired, not really wanting to know but thinking that it might explain the whole situation. It might even help her rationalize it.

"No! It just wasn't working, and I deserve to be happy, sweetheart," her mother acquiesced. "Your father is unhappy, too. Marriage is about making one another happy."

Lucy rolled her eyes and looked out the window. "That's not how marriage works. You can't *make* anyone happy. People *choose* happiness," Lucy replied, remembering words she had read in Grace's journals. "You don't just *need* to move on. You don't get to just quit when things get difficult."

"Lucy, I know it's hard to understand. This is a lot for you to process, but we have grown apart... and neither one of us has been happy. Your dad knows that, even though he can't seem to admit it. I need more. He's just not able to give me what I need," her mom continued, trying to gain her daughter's acceptance of the state of her marriage.

"Why do you think I can't understand? I understand that you GAVE UP and that you DECIDED to quit," Lucy argued, looking at her mom. The energy in the room shifted, as if Lucy struck a nerve. She continued to push back. "Your commitment to each other should mean more than this... LOVE should mean more."

"Lucy!" her mother replied angrily, her voice raised. "I need to be happy in life, too. I can't be expected to be miserable and to live in a marriage that is loveless. Your dad and I want different things in our lives. I'm just... I'm done. You've been at home for the fights. You've heard all of our disagreements. You know that this marriage isn't right and that there's no fixing it"

A Ride Down the Road ©2019

"No," Lucy argued, "I don't know that the marriage won't work. Marriages are supposed to be a forever commitment, In good times and in bad. In sickness and in health. I know you all didn't really try counseling. I know you lied to me about that just so you could sneak off and end it. Mom, this is my life, too! It's like you both snuck off and ended my family."

"Don't be so dramatic," Lucy's mom said, as she rolled her eyes. "You've always been so selfish. You just think about yourself and never about me or about how I feel."

"What?!" exclaimed, dumbfounded by her statement. "Can you *hear* yourself? All you talk about is *your* happiness and *your* needs. You don't have a right to call *me* selfish."

"You are still my child, and you can't talk to me that way," her mother said, glaring at her. She stood up from the bed and shook her finger at Lucy.

Lucy wasn't sure how much more to push. She was angry and disappointed. Before, it was because they were ruining her life, and now, it was because she knew they were ruining their *own* lives.

"Mom, I love you. But I don't agree with you. And I don't want this new life. Can't you keep trying?" Lucy pleaded. She held tight to the blanket in her hand and rubbed the soft edge.

"Lucy, it doesn't matter what you want... this is our life, and you will be coming home with me tomorrow," she said emphatically, as she walked to the door.

"Why? Why is it such a big deal for me to come home with you?" Lucy asked, wanting to scream and start throwing things. She kept pushing her anger down, but it kept boiling back up. Something inside told Lucy that there was more to this story, more to what was being presented.

"Listen, I agreed that you would live with me, and your father agreed to pay my rent for the rest of the year. So I can get on my feet. So I can afford to have a chance at a life," her mother admitted. Lucy stared at her mother. Suddenly, everything came into focus: It was a financial decision. She didn't necessarily want Lucy with her, she just needed the money.

"I am *not* your golden ticket!" Lucy exploded. "I am 17 years old, and you can't force me to leave. I will call and talk to Dad maybe you all can work out some other type of arrangement, but I am not a pawn for your financial gain."

Her mom slammed the door so hard that it bounced back open, stomping loudly down the hallway. Lucy heard her shrill voice all the way from the kitchen as she complained to Grandma.

"Mom! She does not understand! I can't afford to live on my own without that money. Her father agreed to pay me extra but only if she lived with me. This is my chance to start fresh and do what I want to do, for once in my life!" she screamed desperately.

"Dear, can you hear yourself? I don't know who you are right now, but this is not who I raised. I don't know what or who has gotten into your head that makes you think this is all right," Grandma snapped. Lucy had never heard her speak like that before. She thought back to their conversation earlier in the summer about letting your adult children make their decisions, even when it hurts to watch them suffer.

"And what about Lucy?" Grandma added, her tone softening. "You were given this gift of a beautiful daughter. God blessed you with her, after all those years of not being able to conceive."

"I deserve *happiness*," her mother cried. "I don't want to be married any longer! I don't want to be a mother. I don't want to have to carry that burden any longer. I… I just want to be free."

A Ride Down the Road ©2019

"Oh, my sweet girl," Grandma's voice broke. "We *deserve* nothing."

"How can you *say* that?" wailed Lucy's mother.

Grandma's voice cut through the tears as she pleaded with her daughter. "Colleen, the path you are on only leads to pain."

Lucy got up from the bed and closed the door. She didn't want to hear anymore. She didn't want to think any more about what all of this meant or of how she was being used. She picked up the journal and looked at its worn cover. Grace had taken a path that led to pain. Her choices took her away from God's best for her. She saw how Laura and Christopher represented God's love in welcoming her back. Lucy struggled with the idea of that as she felt like she just wanted her mom to go away.

"God, I don't know how to forgive if she ever changes. I can't even *imagine* her ever changing. But maybe someday. Help me. Help me forgive. Help me," Lucy prayed.

Outside, she heard the familiar sound of Tucker's truck. She grabbed her knapsack and stuffed her sketchpad and journal inside. She quickly dressed and threw on her ball cap.

She walked into the kitchen and saw her mother sitting at the table, her shoulders shaking and her head buried in her arms. Lucy didn't want to engage her. She didn't really want to even see her. She quickly grabbed a couple of biscuits and walked past her.

"Lucy," her mother pleaded, looking up. Her face was red from crying. Lucy ignored her and headed for the front door. She found Tucker and Grandma talking in hushed tones next to the porch swing.

"Grandma, I'll be back later," she called, brushing past them.

"Hey, there," Tucker said, sounding confused. She hurried down the path to the truck. He gave Grandma a quick hug, then ran to catch up with Lucy.

"Can we go?" she asked, but it didn't seem much like a question. She wasn't sure if she would cry or scream.

"Go?" he asked. "Sure… uh… sure, let's go!"

He opened the truck door for her and she got in without making eye contact. Lucy was convinced that if she looked at him, she would start crying. She stared straight ahead as he joined her in the truck. They drove down the dirt road, and Lucy observed the fields that surrounded them. The cows and grass that had seemed so lame when she first arrived were now familiar and comforting.

After some time had passed, Tucker asked, "So I'm guessing things didn't go so well with your mom?"

"No," she replied, laying her head against the window, "You know the Bible says we are to respect and obey our parents, but I am not sure how to respect them right now, what with this mess they're making. They are getting divorced because *things aren't working out* and *they just want to be happy*. I mean, really? Really?! They couldn't try to work things out? It's not like either one of them is evil. I lived there, I know! Maybe complacent, maybe boring, but not evil. It's not like one of them is an alcoholic or abusive. She even told me neither one is having an affair! I almost wish one of them would just do something to make me hate them and move on!"

She continued to ramble on about her parents, and Tucker listened quietly. He took an unfamiliar turn down a dirt road that lead to a dead end and parked the truck. They sat there, facing an ominous looking tree line.

"Come on," he said, getting out and waiting for her in front of the truck. She sat for a moment, wondering what he was doing, then got out to join him.

"What are we doing here?" she asked, surveying the tree line in front of them. It looked impenetrable, as if the trees were a line of soldiers charged with keeping unwanted guests from entering.

"Let's go for a walk," he said, starting to walk away. She stood at the front of the truck and watched him saunter off, wondering if she'd said too much. He turned and motioned for her to join him. She paused a few moments longer, then ran to catch up with him.

They entered the forest through a hidden path. It was overgrown and heavily wooded. Small shrubs dangerously peeked out from the ground, weeds latched on to Lucy's socks, and the tree roots seemed to grab her feet. She tripped, grabbing on to the branches of a nearby tree to catch herself before she hit the ground.

"This path is dangerous," she said warily.

"You'll be fine, just come on. I promise you it's worth it at the end," called Tucker, not even looking back at her. Tucker pulled up some of the tall weeds and knocked down the branches that would be in her way. The path, getting more and more rocky, turned sharply and became steep. He reached down to help her with the ascent.

"Where are we going?" Lucy asked, wiping her hands off on her shorts after climbing up a particularly rocky incline.

"Sometimes, good things don't come easy," he chuckled, reaching back again to help her up another set of slippery rocks. "It'll be worth it. Just come on."

They hiked for what felt like an hour until they came to a man-made clearing that overlooked the lake. The town was no longer in sight, just hills and water. It was magnificent. A large tree laid on its side close to the cliff's edge. Tucker walked over and sat down, taking in the view, and Lucy plopped down next to him with a big sigh.

"Where are we?" she asked in amazement. Lucy had grown to love Table Rock Lake. She loved how it snaked through the Ozark mountains and created hidden coves and quiet areas.

"This is my spot. I come here to think and pray," he said, still looking at the view, the water slightly visible through the trees. "It's hard to believe that all this beauty was created to stop flooding," he mused.

"Really?" Lucy asked. Boats sped across the water, looking like little bugs, their wake rolling behind them all the way to the water's edge. Other boats would cut across it, the split wakes rippling through one another, creating new patterns and sending water in all directions.

"Yes, the Corps of Engineers built a damn because the White River flooded so often. People were wanting a recreation spot, and they kept it nice by keeping people too close to the edge. The Corps eventually bought the land back from the people, and if they didn't want to sell it, they were forced to move. There wasn't an option to stay. The water was coming regardless of whether or not people wanted it to come. On occasion, the water line still rises. It was a big deal in the 50s. Change was inevitable," Tucker said. He picked up a small rock and threw it over the edge of the cliff. Lucy looked up at her new friend as he looked off into the distance. "All of that to say, we enjoy it now… we love the beauty of it… we love going to play on the water, but, originally, a lot of people lost their homes."

Tucker took her hand and explained, "Pain often leads to beauty. Things that don't make sense will someday become clear. God's plan, His timing, and His way always have a purpose. I know it's crazy in a world like we live in. People make bad choices. Even people that we love, and, today, it seems like a flood. It's devastating. But someday, you may see what started as a horrendous flood turn into something beautiful."

A Ride Down the Road ©2019

She nodded. More than that, she understood what he was trying to tell her. After all, a summer with her grandma had once seemed like an awful way to spend her last summer before college, but it had become one of the best times of her life. Now, all she wanted was wanted to stay.

"I get what you're saying, Tucker. I really do. But... I don't want to leave," she said, her eyes begging him to fix the situation. "My mom just wants me to live with her so she can get money from my dad."

"I don't want you to leave, either," he replied, looking back at the water, carefully putting his arm around her shoulders as he continued, "With your mom, I want you to always keep the door open. I mean, in your heart. Someday, she may choose a different path. I know it's hard. I had to deal with a lot with my dad."

They sat for hours, talking about writing one another and keeping in touch.

"By the way, how did your mom come across the journal?" Lucy asked, as they carefully hiked back down to the truck.

"Albert is my step-dad," Tucker answered nonchalantly, extending his hand to help her across some loose rocks.

"What? Albert? Are you serious?! How has *that* not come up until now?!" Lucy said, throwing her hands in the air.

"You never asked," he laughed, grabbing her arm as she started to slip. "Careful! Want me to tell you how it ends?" he asked.

"No way!" she replied with a grin, then continued, "But I was surprised by the part I read last night, the part about how the church reacted."

"Yes, there was a lot to learn," Tucker replied. The two began to discuss it as they cautiously followed the steep path down the hill.

I dread this Sunday morning. I woke up and longed to stay in bed. It's not because I love the Lord less than before. It's that people can be so cruel. I am starting to show. I hear the whispers. People talk about me as if I can't understand or hear. A few of them came to the house last night to speak with Christopher. They told him in hushed tones that maybe I should stay home until the baby arrives. James' family does not accept me because I am poor... orphaned... worthless. The church cannot accept me because I have sinned, which, in their eyes, makes me worthless. I wonder if, were my sin less obvious, they would consider it less sinful. Yet Laura and Christopher have shown me that the way the church is acting doesn't line up with the Word of God. It says nothing of the sort! I know it would be easier on them to not see me, not be faced with someone who has made a mistake, but here I am. I just don't know what to do.

It had been a month since Grace returned home from Springfield. She was finally past all of the morning sickness, but the relief of that was clouded by the challenge of trying to hide the pregnancy. Over the last few weeks, everything had fallen into the same routine: Teaching and preaching. Eating and Laughing. Being a family just like before.

David had come to dinner several times over the course of a few weeks, and, of course, on Sundays. He hadn't said a word again about marriage or even how he felt for Grace. He just showed up and treated her as he had before anyone knew about the baby. They would find ways to go out on the porch and talk about everything and nothing.

One particular Sunday, Grace dragged herself out of bed and walked to church early so she could watch the world wake up. The birds were singing to each other, the squirrels were running up and down the trees, and the sun was cresting the hill. Creation was glorifying its Creator. How could the same God who made all of this beauty take the time to care about her and her problems? She remembered Laura telling her that God knit her together in her mother's womb and numbered the hairs on her head. That if He clothes the lilies of the field in splendor and feeds the birds of the air, how much more will he care for her? She breathed in the clean morning air and breathed out her troubles as she walked up to the church.

Grace sat on a bench, watching the kids play as they laughed and chased each other. Each one would come up to her to get a kiss on their head and words of praise. She loved them all. She thought about how she cared so much for each one of them and was reminded again of her walk to church. God made each one of those kids special and beautiful. He has a plan and a purpose for each one of them, always wanting what's best for them.

"Ms. GRAAACE!" Albert yelled, interrupting her meditation. He jumped out of the truck and ran to her, stopping just before he reached her to give her a gentle hug. "Soft touches," he said quietly, reminding himself of his Dad's instructions.

"Hello, my sweet boy! "How are you?" she asked, cupping his freckled cheeks in her hands.

"I am good," he replied, as Ben came up behind them. Ben gently leaned over and gave her a shy hug.

"Are you doing ok, Ms. Grace?" he asked. Grace always thought of him as a shepherd, he was always looking after those around him.

"I am good, sweet boy," she replied, "You boys go play. Run off some energy before we have to go inside." They boys sped off to play with the other children before the service started.

David stood next to the truck, talking to Christopher. The men both looked concerned. Christopher looked at the ground and shook his head. Grace wondered what they were discussing. Then David put both hands on Christopher's shoulders and bowed his head. It looked like they might be praying. When they finished, Christopher

A Ride Down the Road ©2019

went into the church, and David made his way to Grace. He smiled at her as he sat next to her on the bench.

"Good morning," she said, delighted that he had come over to see her. "Is Christopher ok?"

David nodded, then said softly, "I know you overheard the people who stopped by their house last night to talk. Christopher told me about it this morning." He looked grieved.

"Maybe they are right, David," she replied, looking at her feet and digging her shoe into the dirt. It had broken her heart to hear them talk about her the night before, but it made her feel even worse that Christopher felt like he had to defend her. He had countered each of their objections with scripture, insisting that the church must be welcoming to everyone that it was the only biblical response.

"But am I really that different now? It's not like I am saying that what I did was right. But am I such an awful example that I should just stay hidden away?" Grace asked.

"No," David said, his voice soft and gentle as he reached over and took her hand. "Jesus didn't act like that. He told people to bring their broken. He ate with tax collectors and talked with the woman at the well. Church is supposed to be a group of people trying to live in a way that reflects Him and helping each other along the way."

"But I didn't do that. I didn't make a decision that reflects Him, quite the opposite, and now I have a constant reminder of it. It does not matter what I do, going forward, my poor choice will always be visible, always be subject to someone else's opinion," she said, rubbing her growing baby bump.

"Grace, God's opinion is the only one that matters," he began, when Christopher walked out onto the steps and rang the bell, signaling everyone to come inside.

"We should go," she said, standing up and eyeing the door nervously.

David stood, then leaned down to whisper in her ear, "You are worthy to be here, just like anyone else. This is where you should be. That's what you told me when we met the very first time, and I started coming after that. You know why? Because you were right."

Grace smiled back at him, grateful. David always knew what to say to touch her heart.

The service started with a song, as it usually did. Christopher led them in Amazing Grace, a crowd favorite, and the congregation sang loudly through all the verses.

Amazing Grace
How Sweet the Sound
That saved a wretch like me
I once was lost but now I'm found
was blind but now I see.

Christopher straightened his notes a few times, then folded them and put them back in his pocket. He stared out at the crowd, his eyes scanning the room as if he were searching for something in particular. Grace couldn't tell what he was looking for, but the room became eerily still as he waited. Finally, after an uncomfortable silence, he opened his Bible and began to read.

John 8:1-12
Jesus went unto the mount of Olives. And early in the morning He came again into the temple, and all the people came unto Him; and He sat down and taught them. And the scribes and Pharisees brought unto him a woman taken in adultery; and when they had set her in the midst, they said unto Him, Master, this woman was taken in adultery, in the very act. Now Moses in the law commanded us that such should be stoned: but what sayest Thou? This they said, tempting Him, that they might have to accuse Him.

A Ride Down the Road ©2019

*But Jesus stooped down, and with His finger wrote on the ground, as though He heard them not. So when they continued asking Him, He lifted up Himself, and said unto them, **He that is without sin among you, let him first cast a stone at her.***

And again He stooped down, and wrote on the ground. And they which heard it, being convicted by their own conscience, went out one by one, beginning at the eldest, even unto the last: and Jesus was left alone, and the woman standing in the midst.

When Jesus had lifted up Himself, and saw none but the woman, He said unto her, Woman, where are those thine accusers? hath no man condemned thee?

She said, No man, Lord. And Jesus said unto her, Neither do I condemn thee: go, and sin no more.

Then spake Jesus again unto them, saying, I am the light of the world: he that followeth me shall not walk in darkness, but shall have the light of life.

Christopher set his Bible down on the pulpit, again staring into the audience, his eyes filling with tears. Grace thought he might break down in front of everyone.

After a long silence, he began to speak.

"The scripture, over and over, implores us… NO… *demands* that we examine our hearts, constantly evaluating how we compare to Jesus. Why? When we know that there is no one equal to the son of God. He was perfect in all He said and did while He was on this earth. We are to examine ourselves to remind… not *just* remind… but to position ourselves in humility. Our sin, whether the world considers it big or inconsequential, would have been enough to still nail Him to the cross. One sin! One thought of malice, one word of disdain, stealing one piece of candy from a store -- *any* one of those sins would separate us from God Himself. Our sin is the great equalizer. No man is greater than any other,

A Ride Down the Road ©2019

because we have all e sinned and fallen short of God's glory.

We must realize that, to Jesus, no sin is greater than another -- it *all* separates us from God. Some people say that He was writing in the dirt the sins of those surrounding the woman. Others say he was writing the names of God. Regardless of what it was that He was writing, His words were clear. 'Those among you without sin, cast the first stone. Those among you who can stand without fault, without separation from God Almighty, *you* take the judgement seat of God and *you* make the decisions on who is to be accepted and not accepted into God's glory.'

When all of those who judged her dropped their stones and walked away. He said to the woman, 'Where are your accusers? Where are those who thought themselves so above you that they wanted to rid this world of you?'

His words challenge us all. Where are those who don't realize that our sin makes us equally lost? We are all fallen people, damaged and broken. We gather each week to learn, to encourage, to connect and have fellowship with our brothers and sisters. But brothers and sisters, this is a house of God's love. This is a house that believes in second. Nay, third, fourth, fifth -- SEVENTY times seven chances in the pursuit of serving this world in Jesus name!! In the pursuit of being a reflection of God's love to a lost world! If we cannot love one another, the people of this church, in a way that reflects God's love, then how, beloved sisters and brothers, will we *ever* love a lost world in the way that reflects Jesus?! Our responsibility is to respond rightly is greater than that of those in this world, because we have salvation in Jesus Christ. Our calling is greater than their ability to reject, hate, judge, and shun. Our calling is to become a conduit of the love of Jesus to a lost and hurting world. I know that is who we are as a family of believers. I know that is who each and every one of you are... "

Grace sat with tears streaming down her face. She reached into her pocket and pulled out a small, white handkerchief, using its scalloped edge to dry her tears. Suddenly, it all became so clear. She realized that she was loved, and would always be loved by God, regardless of her choices, despite her betrayal of her commitment to Him. From that day on, something in Grace changed. She gained confidence, knowing that she was a beloved child of God. She finally understood her value and worth. That she was adopted not only into Laura and Christopher's family, but also into the family of Jesus Christ Himself. It finally all made sense to her. It finally all became *real*.

~ Chapter 19 ~

Lucy returned home to find her grandma sitting alone on the front porch swing. Tucker stopped the truck and they sat for a moment.

"Did your mom leave?" he asked, looking around but not seeing her car.

"I don't know," Lucy replied, staring at the barn where she first heard her parents fight. "Listen, I don't know what's going to happen, but I promise I won't leave without saying goodbye."

"Just call me if you need anything," he said. "If, for some reason, you can't say goodbye in person, it's ok. I have a phone, and we can write, too."

"I'll see you later," she said, letting herself out of the truck. She walked up the brick pathway to the porch and sat down next to her grandma. Lucy laid her head on her shoulder, and they sat in silence as Tucker backed out of the driveway and drove away.

"When am I leaving?" Lucy asked, as she inhaled the sweet smell of her grandma's rosewater perfume. Lucy reached over and held her hand.   Her grandma's skin was paper-thin and soft. The veins on top of her hand popped up like mountain ranges, all in a light shade of blue. When she was a child, she would try to push them back into her skin to make them disappear.

"You are staying," Grandma replied, sighing. Lucy's head popped up. She was amazed, excited, and confused.

"What! Just like that? What happened?" Lucy asked, nearly unable to contain herself. She stared into her grandma's sullen face.

"Lucy, your mom has a lot of things to work out," Grandma replied. "She has made some choices... selfish choices... and we discussed that now is a good time for her to go figure those things out. Now is also a good time for *you* to stay *here* and finish school."

Grandma stopped talking as she wiped away a tear. "No one wants to see their child suffer, regardless of their culpability in the issue. We all want them to grow up, make good decisions, and live out all the things we taught them," she continued, gently touching Lucy's cheek. "Your grandfather would say: Our job is just to raise them up in the way they should go and hide God's word in their heart. We can't make them follow, we can't make them believe, we can't live their life for them. Once we launch them from the safety of our home, then our responsibility shifts to fervent prayer..."

Her voice broke, and she stopped. They sat there in silence, watching the dusk morph into the night sky.

Lucy knew that Grandma considered her children as her life's work, that they were everything to her. Grandma saw the wisdom in what Grandpa said, that was clear, but Lucy wondered if it were harder to really *believe* it in her heart. It was difficult for Lucy to see her grandma hurting. She wanted her to know that it was nothing *she* did, that her mom was just stubborn and hard-headed sometimes. It broke Lucy's heart to see her grandma suffer. She knew her grandma's heart must be broken, too, watching her daughter make bad choices and experience the painful consequences.

When the stars came out, they went inside, Lucy to a plate of leftover meatloaf and Grandma to her bed without supper. She looked more worn than usual.

As Lucy microwaved her leftovers, she wondered how Grace's story might take shape. She grabbed the journal as she sat down at the table to eat. Only 2 pages left.

I keep going over in my mind this idea of marrying David. He has never stopped being there for me since we came home. He has showed up almost daily to eat with our family, I am starting to wonder if his kitchen is broken or if he just can't cook. I know that he is a good man and a good father. Why didn't I see this before? He is my best friend, and I am glad his kitchen is broken...

It was the last day of school, and Grace got up early to help Laura in the kitchen. They made biscuits and gravy for the family.

"Laura," Grace said, washing the yellow Pyrex bowl to free it from leftover flour. "What if I *did* marry David?"

Laura stopped rolling the dough, looking surprised at the question. She paused before she replied, "Well, what if you *did*? What would that look like for you?"

Laura's common technique of turning a question back to the questioner always made Grace smile. The women were silent for a while as Grace considered her response.

"I would get to live *this* life," Grace said, reaching for her towel and drying the bowl. She looked out the window at the sun as it crested the trees behind the house.

"Would that be all?" Laura asked, pulling out the round biscuit cutter and gently punching out biscuits. "Would it just be this wonderful, normal life that we all share? Or would it be more?"

Grace considered her questions and continued, "I just can't get over what a burden I would be for him. You all have never made me feel that way, but I know that's what I am."

"You are *not* a burden… you are a *gift*. You were brought here for a reason in this specific time and this specific place. You have *never* been a burden or anything like that. James Carter filled your head with lies! Or maybe he just exploited your greatest fears in life," Laura went on, pulling out

A Ride Down the Road ©2019

perfectly round biscuits and setting them on the pan. "Grace, you are not a burden to anyone. We are all adults here and can make our own decisions on what is and is not worth having in our lives. You never have been a burden. You are our *family*."

Grace set the bowl down and walked over to hug her cousin, her heart welling up with gratitude. She realized that the *family* she had always wanted was something she already *had*, without even realizing it. Everything she wanted was always right here.

They finished the biscuits, and Grace set off for school. When she got there, the classroom was already filling up with students. Albert and Ben were the last to arrive, and Albert had a handful of wildflowers that he had picked from the side of the road.

"Sorry we are late, but I picked these for you," Albert said proudly, handing them to her with a big, toothless grin.

"Albert, where are your teeth?!" Grace laughed, taking his freckled cheeks in her hands. "You have holes in your mouth!"

Albert stuck his tongue through the hole and scrunched his nose. "They came out! And I got *money* for them, too!"

"Really?" Grace said, accepting his gift and releasing him back to his seat.

"So we are not tardy?" he asked sheepishly, grinning at her again.

"No, you are still tardy. Now go sit down." He sighed loudly as he stomped to his seat. She raised her eyebrows at him, and he quickly apologized, turning his eyes to the floor. Ben smacked his arm and gave him a look that said, "I told you so!"

A Ride Down the Road ©2019

"Let's get started, class," Grace said loudly, clapping her hands. The day seemed to fly by, and the students, anticipating the start of summer, could hardly stay in their seats. There were side conversations all day about time at the river and vacations. Many had plans for leisure and rest; others had summer full of farm work to look forward to. The day finally ended, and Grace dismissed the class. She stood at the back door to hug each student as they left and told them to make sure to come to church so she could see them throughout the summer.

"Dad is at Pastor's house working on something. Can we walk home with you?" Ben asked, as they came up for their goodbye hug.

"Yes, of course," she replied, tussling Albert's hair. Grace smiled as she thought about how nice it would be to see David today and to sit and talk with him.

Soon, the trio left and walked down the dirt road towards the house. They laughed, played tag, admired the clouds, and even picked more flowers. As they neared the house, Albert slipped his plump hand into Grace's and looked up at her with his snaggle-tooth grin.

"I love you, Ms. Grace," he said. "I am going to miss you this summer."

"Me, too, Albert. Maybe your kitchen will still be broken and you can come eat with us," she replied, wondering for a moment what it would be like to be his mom, to be with him every day and enjoy his sweet, freckled face.

"Our kitchen isn't broken," Ben said casually, then suddenly tagged Albert and ran ahead with a yell. "You're it, Toothless Wonder!"

As Grace neared the house, she saw David and Christopher leaning against the green truck, talking. Laura walked out of the house carrying a plate full of cookies in one hand and the baby on her hip. The boys raced around the oak tree

A Ride Down the Road ©2019

squealing with delight.   Grace stood and soaked it all in.
Normal. This was just normal and wonderful. And normal
was just perfect. Normal was all Grace ever wanted or
needed.

Laura spotted her and raised the large plate, nodding for her
to join them.

"Grace!" she said, "I made your favorite peanut butter!"

Grace walked towards them, breathing in the warm summer
air.   David smiled as he opened the back of the truck. She
sat there with Laura, enjoying the cookies and conversation.
They shared about their day, laughed at the boy's antics,
and snuggled the giggling baby. When the baby started to
fuss, Christopher took him from Laura.

"Smells like a change is needed," Christopher said, holding
the baby out in front of him.   He turned and quickly walked
back to the house. "Laura!" he called, "I am going to need
some moral support."

"Well, that means he wants me to change the baby," she
laughed, taking the plate of half-eaten cookies and walking
to the house. "Dinner will be done shortly!"

"So you had a good last day of school?" David asked Grace,
sitting down next to her in the truck.

"Yes, the kids were ready to be done. They all have summer
plans and that's all they have thought about for days," Grace
replied, as she watched the boys run in the yard. Tag had
changed to cops and robbers. They were carefree and
laughing every time they captured someone.

"David, I need to ask you something," Grace said soberly,
looking straight at him.

"Ok," he replied, smiling at her, "I prefer sugar cookies next
time." They both laughed as he nudged her shoulder. "Not
the question?" he laughed.

A Ride Down the Road ©2019

"No," Grace said slowly. She hesitated, then looked up at him. "When you said that you wanted to marry me, was it because you were trying to help save me from the humiliation of being pregnant out of wedlock?" She worried that his response would be a simple "yes" that his offer had been nothing more than just a solution to her problem.

The smile fell from his face as he shook his head. "Grace, falling in love with someone -"

Grace held her hands up as she interrupted, "But, you offered to marry me, and I know it was partly to save me."

"No," he said, standing up quickly. "Grace, I want to marry you because I look forward to every moment I get to spend with you. I wake up each day trying to figure out how to get all of my work done so that I can come here for a meal. The kitchen works fine at my house, I just want to see you. I love your smile, love to hear your voice..."

Grace couldn't help but smile as he spoke. "David," she started, but he interrupted.

"No, I see you. The beautiful, caring, kind woman who tripped on the steps of the train and fell into my arms on the first day you arrived. I see you for who you are, and I want you in my life. This mistake that you think *defines* you is just something you did, it's not who you are. I don't care what people think or say. This, what we have right here, the kids playing, sitting together, talking in the truck, having dinner with our friends, all these normal things! *This* is what I want for my life, and I want you in it. I told you that I will be patient and I will, but I love you. I wish you could just believe me."

"David!" Grace said, smiling, "I believe you, and I love you too. I do, I love you too."

"You love me?" he asked, surprised by her admission. David wrapped his arms around her and picked her up, swinging her around. Both of them were completely elated.

A Ride Down the Road ©2019

"I will marry you. If you will still have me. I want this life too. I love you," she said, staring into his eyes. David leaned down and kissed her.

"Dad! What are you doing?" Albert yelled. Both boys stood with mouths wide open, stunned.

"He is getting married," Christopher's voice boomed from the front porch.

"Yes, we are!" David called back to the family, then leaned down and kissed Grace again. "Yes, we are."

~ Chapter 20 ~

Lucy knocked at the round wooden door. The house was a large Tudor that looked like something out of a designer magazine. Grandma held on to her arm for balance with one hand and was carrying a gift bag in the other. It was fall, and the leaves on the trees were starting to change, framing the view with majestic color. The porch steps were lined with white, green, and orange pumpkins and gourds. A small black settee with a "Happy Fall, Y'all" sign on it looked inviting. Even though it was made of iron, it seemed fragile. It was another "treasure" that Kary had reclaimed and repaired.

The door opened, and there stood Albert. He was dressed simply, wearing a blue flannel shirt that had notes sticking out of the pocket. He was still freckled but all of his hair was gone.

"Hello, Grandma!" he said. His blue eyes smiled as he stepped out and hugged her gently. "Lucy, great to see you!" He opened the door wide to welcome her in. "Please, come in!"

It was almost unreal to meet the little boy from the stories she had grown to love. He carefully took her grandma's hand and guided her into the house.

"Kary, our guests are here!" he called, as they walked through the entryway into the family room. The room had a menagerie of painted furniture and adorable vignettes. One red shelf was full of old tin globe banks with blue books. Another had antique cameras and jars of marbles.

A large black lab waddled up to them, nudging Lucy to pet him. He had speckles of white across his chin like the beard of an old man, and it looked like he was smiling.

"That's Boomer," she heard Ethan's voice from the couch. "He is safe, you can pet him."

Lucy knelt and petted her friend. "Hello, Booms!" she said to the dog. "Are you good?"

Kary hurried through the room, stopping quickly to kiss Grandma, and rushed straight to the kitchen.

"Dinner will be ready soon," Kary said, "I got caught up in a book I was reading. It was sooo good. The author's name is Ashlynn something or other… I don't know. But it was so good!"

"Can I do anything to help, dear?" Grandma asked, as Albert took her jacket for her.

"No, no just sit. I am good!" Kary replied. She danced through the kitchen, preparing food and setting out plates. "You know, it tastes better if it looks good on the serving plates," she joked.

Grandma and Lucy found seats in the family room, and Albert joined them.

"So, how is school going Lucy?" he asked.

"It's good! Everything transferred, and I am on track to graduate. I applied for college in the Springfield area so I could be close to Grandma. One is as far as Bolivar, but it's not too far." Lucy replied, as the dog came up and sat next to her feet. He let out a sigh and laid his head on her lap.

"Boomer," Albert said starting to get up.

Lucy scratched the dog's ears and said, "It's ok, the Booms and I are friends. Tucker brings him to the farm sometimes."

Kary opened the back door yelled, "Tucker! Lunch time!"

Albert shook his head as he looked at Kary. "You know, I hung that huge triangle bell thing out there so that you don't have to yell."

"I know. I am sorry. I was just in a hurry. Ethan, please come in here, and we'll set the table," Kary said, as Ethan reluctantly got up and sauntered to the kitchen. The door swung open and Tucker came in, his arms full of split wood. He closed the door carefully with his foot.

"Kary, we are not in a rush," Grandma said, smiling. "I am glad to get out of the house for some time with friends."

"Hi, everyone," Tucker said, carefully putting the pieces of wood next to the fireplace in an empty, cast-iron bucket.

"It's too hot for a fire, but I think it makes the room look more inviting to at least have wood in there," Kary said, as she carried serving dishes to the table, then ushered everyone to the table.

"I'll say the blessing," Albert said, opening his hands on either side. Lucy took hold of one and Tucker grabbed the other. "Dear Lord, we are so thankful for all of the many blessings in our lives. We are so thankful for family and friends. Please let this time be filled with uplifting connection to one another. Let us encourage each other on our life's journey. We ask that You bless each person at this table, and bless the food we are about to eat. Amen." He lightly squeezed Lucy's hand.

"So, I have news!" Tucker announced, as people started to pass the serving plates, "I got accepted to Southwest Baptist University AND they offered me a scholarship to play baseball!"

Everyone clapped and cheered. "I already knew," Kary said smiling as she scooped salad onto her plate, "but it's fun to celebrate again."

A Ride Down the Road ©2019

She passed the salad bowl and continued, "I am just excited that there is a Starbucks on the way to the school. I also heard there is a good little coffee shop in Bolivar. You know, priorities."

"What will you study?" Grandma asked, as Lucy dipped food from the serving dish onto her plate.

"Well, I was thinking about business, but have been talking a lot to our pastor, and now I'm thinking maybe ministry. I may double major, though," he said, smiling. "A lot of pastors are bi-vocational now."

It seemed hard to believe that they were both two months into their senior year. Ever since she officially moved in to live with Grandma, they had enjoyed many conversations on the hill, overlooking the lake, talking about the future and what it might hold. Lucy knew Tucker was considering ministry, and she encouraged him to pursue that path. He was clearly made for it. No one had ever been able to speak so clearly about God's word to her in the way he did.

The end of the summer had been a whirlwind. Lucy's father brought her clothes and spent a few days with her. She took him to the house with three gables and shared all of her adventures. He loved it. He apologized for the mess he had made of his marriage, admitting that he wished he had been more attentive to her mother. Even though her mom eventually confessed that she was seeing someone else, he never spoke disparagingly of her. He was devastated by their failure to work things out and stay married. He blamed himself. Both of her parents agreed it would be best for Lucy to stay with Grandma through her senior year. Her father made her promise that she would call every day. He had made several trips for visits all ready.

"I heard you read my mother's journals and letters," Albert said, smiling as he took another helping of potatoes.

"Yes," she said, getting up from the table and getting the gift bag, "I brought them for you. I also made you something as a thank-you for letting me read them."

She handed the gift bag to Albert, who reached into the bag and carefully pulled out a frame made of old barn wood. Inside the frame was a hand-drawn picture of the old, green truck. He smiled as he touched the picture, then held it up for Kary to see.

"It's beautiful," he said. "You know, you could say that old truck brought them together. Their love for each other developed over time as they took rides down the road. It's a special vehicle."

"Kind of like us," Kary said, as she started to get up from the table.

"In the truck?" Albert laughed, "I don't think so…"

"Well, it wasn't that *truck*," Kary smiled, resting her chin on her hand. "Later in life, David upgraded. In 1968, he bought a brand-new black Camaro convertible. Albert was driving that when we met. Not that I wouldn't have fallen in love with Albert if all he had was an old green truck, but the flashy Camaro *did* help his case… "

"Come with me," Albert said, tapping Lucy's arm. He got up from the table and walked into the family room, pulling an old picture album from the bookshelf. They made their way to the couch and sat down together and thumbed through the book.

There were pictures of the school, and Albert explained how Grace had taught there for years, until it eventually closed and the kids were sent to the larger school in nearby Reed Springs.

Then Albert turned the page to pictures of Ben in high school. He explained how Ben had become a missionary to

A Ride Down the Road ©2019

Korea after his time in the service. There was also a picture of a large family, seated in a church pew, lined up by height. There were 8 of them total in the row, Grace and David on one end, and their youngest at the other end of the line-up. The couple sat hand-in-hand, beaming with pride. Albert named off all of the kids in order, then went back and pointed at the beautiful girl sitting next to him. He paused as he gently put his finger on the picture.

"That's Hope," he said softly. "Hope is the baby that Grace had soon after she married my Dad. I can't tell you what a joy she was to have in my life. She was funny and kind. Intelligent and amazing."

"Was?" Lucy asked. "Has she passed away?"

"Yes, she died in an accident when she was in college." Albert said, "We were heartbroken. She was studying to become a teacher."

"Whatever happened to James Carter?" Lucy asked, staring at the picture.

"James did become a senator, and he did marry that blonde," Albert said. "But, like most of his marriages, it didn't last long," Albert chuckled.

"How many were there?" Lucy asked.

"Three or four, at least. He was plagued with scandal in his life, but it was all scandal that he created himself," Albert said, "He came to Hope's funeral and spoke to Grace after. He apologized and said she was the one he let get away. Pretty sure my Dad wanted to punch him for showing up, but Grace was kind."

Albert smiled at the picture and continued, "She was always kind. She told him that God had other plans for her life and that she was thankful for those plans. Then, in true Grace

A Ride Down the Road ©2019

form, she shared the gospel with him. He wasn't much interested, just thanked her and left."

Lucy flipped the page and found a picture of Ben dressed in a military outfit, surrounded by all of his siblings and all of Lucy's aunts and uncles. Ben was holding a young Colleen, none other than Lucy's mother.

"That's my mom," she said in surprise, pointing to a young girl who had her arms wrapped around Ben's neck. Her head was on his shoulder.

"Yes, she was always glued to Ben. Lucy, I grew up with your mother. We all went to the same church and did the same things. Our moms hid God's word in our hearts, just as the Bible instructs," Albert said, as he reached over and took her hand. He sighed. "Ultimately, the choices of life are left to the person making them. Life is full of seasons, as my dear wife says. Sometimes, we pick a dark path that leads to a cold season. The good news is there is always a way back and people willing to help."

Lucy nodded as Tucker flopped down on the couch next to her. "Want to go for a ride?" he asked, leaning into her and smiling. Lucy looked over at Grandma for approval.

"Go ahead, dear, I want to talk to Albert and Kary for as long as I can today," Grandma said.

"Ohhh and teach me to make Cherry Mash! I have all the ingredients and you said we could do that today," Kary called from the kitchen as she loaded the dishwasher.

Lucy and Tucker got up to leave, promising to be back in a couple of hours. As they walked out the door onto the porch, Lucy slipped her hand into Tucker's.

"So, it's decided - a pastor, huh?" Lucy asked, looking straight ahead at the green truck parked by the barn.

"Yes, pretty sure that's what God has been trying to tell me," Tucker replied, opening the door for her. He paused for a moment, then added, "You think you could handle that?"

"I could handle that," she replied matter-of-factly, climbing into her seat. He closed the door, ran around to his side and hopped in.

"I have heard *France* needs some pastors...," he said, starting the truck.

"Wait? What?! I thought you wanted to be a *pastor*, not a missionary," she shot back, her eyebrows raised in unbelief.

"Same thing," he shrugged, putting the truck in gear, and heading carefully down the long driveway. They turned on to the road and set out for adventure, talking about everything and nothing -- just as they always did.

A Ride Down the Road ©2019